WIN_S
of
CHA_

Friend or Foe

'Beautiful writing, great character dev...

Stormclouds

'This accurate depiction of violence ... will surprise and educate many. A worthy accomplishment.' *Kirkus Reviews*

Secrets and Shadows

'Heart-stopping action.' *Evening Echo*

Taking Sides

'Dramatic action and storytelling skill.' *Evening Echo*

Across the Divide

'The atmosphere of a troubled city awash with tension and poverty is excellently captured.' *Irish Examiner*

Arrivals

'[Brian Gallagher is] one of Ireland's finest authors of historical fiction for any age ... a consummate storyteller.' *gobblefunked.com*

Pawns

'Riveting and insightful.' *Sunday Independent*

Spies

'Immerses the reader into an Ireland full of Black and Tans, soldiers, rebels, and police informers.' *In Touch Magazine*

Resistance

'An exciting and thrilling adventure story.' *Irish Examiner*

BRIAN GALLAGHER was born in Dublin. He is a full-time writer whose plays and short stories have been produced in Ireland, Britain and Canada. He has worked extensively in radio and television, writing many dramas and documentaries.

Brian is the author of four adult novels, and his other books of historical fiction for young readers are *One Good Turn* and *Friend or Foe* – both set in Dublin in 1916; *Stormclouds,* which takes place in Northern Ireland during the turbulent summer of 1969; *Secrets and Shadows*, a spy novel that begins with the North Strand bombings during the Second World War; *Taking Sides*, about the Irish Civil War; *Across the Divide*, set during the 1913 Lockout, *Arrivals*, a time-slip novel set between modern and early-twentieth-century Ontario; *Pawns* and its sequel, *Spies*, set during Ireland's War of Independence; and *Resistance*, an alternate history set in a Nazi-occupied Ireland. Brian lives with his family in Dublin.

WINDS
of
CHANGE

THREE CHILDREN CAUGHT UP
IN IRELAND'S LAND WAR

BRIAN GALLAGHER

THE O'BRIEN PRESS
DUBLIN

First published 2021 by The O'Brien Press Ltd,
12 Terenure Road East, Rathgar, Dublin 6, D06 HD27, Ireland.
Tel: +353 1 4923333; Fax: +353 1 4922777
E-mail: books@obrien.ie
Website: www.obrien.ie
The O'Brien Press is a member of Publishing Ireland.

ISBN: 978-1-78849-195-2

Printed and bound by Norhaven Paperback A/S, Denmark.
The paper in this book is produced using pulp from managed forests.

Winds of Change receives financial assistance from the Arts Council

Published in:

DEDICATION

To Holly Garrett, bringer of joy into so many lives.

ACKNOWLEDGEMENTS

My thanks to Michael O'Brien for supporting the idea of a novel set at the time of the Land War, to my editor, Helen Carr, for her excellent editing and advice, to publicist Ruth Heneghan for all her efforts on my behalf, to Emma Byrne and Eoin Coveney for their work on cover design, and to everyone at O'Brien Press, with whom it's a pleasure to work.

My thanks also go to Hugh McCusker for his expert proof-reading, to Sylda Langford for her assistance, and to Jonah Dwyer and Ava Hanrahan, two young readers who shared with me their views of an early draft of the story.

My sincere thanks go to Fingal Arts Office for their bursary support, and to the Arts Council for a Professional Development award.

And finally, my deepest thanks are for the constant encouragement of my family, Miriam, Orla, Mark, Holly, Peter and Shelby.

PART ONE

CHANGE IN
THE AIR

CHAPTER ONE

Parkinson Estate, County Westmeath

SATURDAY 9th OCTOBER 1880

Clara Parkinson struggled to control her fear. She clung desperately to the reins as Kaiser, her father's white stallion, galloped wildly through the pine-scented woods. The horse had been startled by the sudden appearance of a stoat, and despite Clara's efforts to rein him in, he was out of control.

'Whoa, Kaiser, whoa!' she cried. Even as she shouted at him, Clara realised that the stallion was beyond heeding her. He was a huge animal, a thoroughbred that stood seventeen hands high, and it was because he was headstrong and temperamental that her father had never allowed Clara to ride him.

Today, though, her parents were visiting friends at Belvedere

House, near Mullingar, and they wouldn't be back until this evening. Clara had taken advantage of their absence to saddle up Kaiser, and she had been enjoying an afternoon canter through the grounds of the family estate when the stoat had burst into her path.

The horse had reared up, then bolted, and Clara had already been smacked in the face by a low-hanging branch. She knew that if she hit a more solid branch at this pace it might be disastrous. Even if she managed to come through unscathed, she could be in big trouble. Disobeying Papa by riding Kaiser was bad enough, but if the horse got injured there would be ructions. Kaiser was a valuable animal, and although her father was a major landowner in County Westmeath, and a wealthy man, he had paid a high price for the stallion. Clara dreaded having to explain herself if the horse broke a leg or otherwise injured himself.

'Whoa, Kaiser, whoa!' she cried again, trying with all her strength to rein him in. But Clara was a slightly built twelve-year-old girl, whereas Kaiser was a fully-grown stallion weighing over eighty stone, and as they careened around a bend in the track the horse ignored her efforts to slow him.

Clara's heart was pounding, but she tried to dampen her fear and think clearly. The longer this went on the greater the chance of a serious accident – she could even be killed if her head smacked into a tree at high speed. Could she jump off the horse, hoping that the woodland floor would break her fall? Maybe. But with the pace at which they were travelling she might break her leg or injure her spine. *Unless she landed in water.* She realised that they were nearing the shore of the small lake at the eastern boundary of the estate. If she freed her feet from the stirrups could she throw herself into the water as they galloped along the shoreline? It would mean getting wet, and she might still hurt herself, but the water would break her fall.

First, though, she had to exit safely from the woods. Despite being jostled by the speed of the bolting horse, Clara tried to stay low in the saddle to avoid low-hanging branches.

'Whoa, Kaiser, whoa, boy!' she shouted again, hoping that eventually her command might get through to the panicking horse.

Instead he continued at speed, then swerved wildly as they reached a sharp bend. His hooves skidded as he hit a muddy patch. Kaiser lost his balance, and Clara screamed as the horse fell. She was thrown from the saddle and catapulted forward. The last thing she saw was a mass of green and gold foliage speeding towards her. Then she hit the ground, and everything suddenly turned black.

Aidan stood motionless in the woods, unsure what to do. He was trespassing on the Parkinson estate, having taken a short cut on the way back to his family's small farm outside the village of Ballydowd. His instinct was to go immediately to the assistance of the girl who had been thrown from the horse. He recognised her as Clara Parkinson, the daughter of the Big House. Although Clara was his own age, he didn't know her, as she didn't socialise with the boys and girls of the village, or the children of her father's tenant farmers. It was said locally that she wasn't snooty, but her family were the gentry, and as such they mixed with people of their own class.

Aidan waited a moment to see if the girl would get up. He hoped she wasn't injured. If she was just shaken, then he would slip away into the woods. But as he watched, there was no sign of her rising, and he became concerned. If she was badly hurt the right thing would be to go to her assistance – even if that meant revealing that he had been trespassing.

But how might she react? Would she report him to her father for being on their land? Aidan knew that people could be unpredictable. Maybe instead of being grateful for his concern she would be embarrassed that he had seen her being thrown from the horse. Maybe she'd resent him for it.

He waited another moment. Still the girl didn't rise. Aidan bit his lip, willing her to get up. But there was no movement, and eventually his conscience took over. He couldn't abandon someone who needed his help. Stepping out from where he had been hiding, he made his way towards the fallen girl. The hazy mid-day sun gave a golden glow to the autumn leaves, but Aidan barely noticed as he approached Clara Parkinson.

She was lying with her eyes closed, and Aidan felt apprehensive. What if she were dead? He could see no blood, however, and he prayed that she had only been knocked unconscious. He dropped to his knees beside her. Just as he leaned over her, she stirred, then blinkingly opened her eyes.

Aidan could see the shock in her expression, and he realised that it must be frightening to awake suddenly and find someone leaning over you.

'What...what are you...?' she began to ask.

'It's all right,' he said reassuringly. 'I saw the horse throw you, and I wanted to make sure you weren't hurt.'

Clara moved her limbs gingerly. 'I...I think I'm all right,' she said.

'Go easy,' Aidan cautioned. 'Just in case you've broken anything.'

Clara carefully sat up. 'I don't...I don't seem to have. But I'm a bit dizzy.'

'Then I wouldn't jump up suddenly. You're a little pale. Give yourself a minute. I'll stay with you till you're all right,' he added, sitting beside her on the forest floor.

'Thank you,' she answered politely.

Her accent was unusual, Aidan thought. She didn't have the local accent, but instead spoke with an English-sounding tone. It was probably influenced by her tutors and her parents, he reasoned. But although she sounded like one of the gentry, and was dressed in what Aidan reckoned was an expensive riding outfit, her manner wasn't condescending.

'I've seen your face before,' she said. 'But I'm sorry, I don't know your name.'

'Aidan. Aidan Daly.'

'I'm Clara,' she said, extending her hand.

'I know,' said Aidan. He thought it was strange to shake hands in these circumstances, but then the gentry probably did lots of things differently, and so he took her outstretched hand, noticing how soft her skin was.

Some of the colour was coming back into Clara's cheeks, and now she looked him directly in the eye. 'How did you come to be here?' she asked.

Aidan felt uncomfortable. 'I…I know I shouldn't have been really. But I was fishing and I took a shortcut home – but I wasn't poaching! I fished in the canal, not the lake on your land.'

'It's all right,' she said,' I'm not going to tell on you.'

Aidan could see that she meant it, and he felt relieved. 'Thanks.'

'Will you do the same for me?'

'How do you mean?'

'I borrowed my father's horse without permission. But if you tell your friends what you saw, they'll tell their parents, and word will get back to Papa. Then I'll be for it.'

'Don't worry, I won't tell a soul.'

'Promise?'

'Cross my heart and hope to die in a barrel of rats!'

Clara burst out laughing, and Aidan liked the way her face lit up when she laughed.

'I've never heard that saying before,' she said

'Really? It just means the promise definitely won't be broken.'

'Then our secrets are safe. Well, that's if I can get Kaiser back to the stables uninjured.'

'That should be all right,' said Aidan, 'he got up after he fell. I saw him grazing at the edge of the woods; we can pick him up on the way back to Ballydowd.'

'Excellent,' said Clara, then she rose carefully to her feet.

Aidan rose also. 'Feeling all right now?' he asked.

'Yes, thank you.' Clara looked at him. 'So, *on a separate note*, as my governess likes to say – did you catch any fish?'

The question was so unexpected that Aidan found himself smiling. 'Yes…I did.'

'What did you get?'

'Some bream and a couple of brown trout.'

'I'd love to catch a fish,' said Clara.

'Have you never?'

'No.'

'Why not?'

'To quote my governess again. *Ladies don't fish!*'

'But you're only – what? Twelve? Thirteen?'

'Twelve. But I'm supposed to be a lady one day. Though that's just rubbish.'

'Being a lady?'

'No, that's fine. Well, some of it's actually a bit silly. But the rest of it's all right. What's rubbish is saying that you can't learn to fish because one day you're going to be a lady.'

'Right.'

'Is it hard to catch fish?'

'Not if you know the right tricks,' said Aidan.

'What are they?'

'Knowing the best bait. Using the right gear. Knowing the best spots.'

Clara thought for moment, then looked enquiringly at Aidan. 'Would you show me how?'

Aidan hesitated. The Land War was causing conflict all across Ireland as small farmers and landlords clashed over fair rents and an end to evictions. The Parkinsons were generally regarded as decent landlords, but Aidan knew there were people who would object strongly to a friendship between members of the opposing classes.

'Only if you want to,' said Clara.

'It's not that I don't want to. It would be fun, but...'

'What?'

'If we're seen together you might get into trouble. And so might I.'

Clara spoke with a hint of mischief in her eyes. 'Then we'd have to make sure we weren't seen, wouldn't we?'

Aidan was tempted to agree. Yet he knew instinctively that this could lead to problems.

Clara smiled and raised an eyebrow. 'Well?'

Aidan hesitated another moment, then acted on impulse. 'All right,' he said, returning her smile.

'Great! When can we do it?'

'When would you like?'

'How about tomorrow?'

Aidan found her enthusiasm infectious, and he grinned. 'OK then. Tomorrow it is!'

CHAPTER TWO

Ashtown, Dublin 15

WEDNESDAY 19th FEBRUARY 2020

Garrett Byrne sat immobile, gripped by curiosity. He was at a desk in his bedroom, a laptop open before him as he studied the screen. He was trying to trace his family roots for a school project and for the last hour he had been looking up old census forms online. Normally he was mildly interested in history, and he had enjoyed several books of historical fiction from the library, but this was different. The fact that it was his own family whose past he was exploring changed things, and he had almost felt like a detective as he followed the trail of ancestors back to the early years of the twentieth century.

He looked now at the scanned 1911 census form and marvelled at the beautiful handwriting of Thomas Donnelly, his ancestor. *Thomas Donnelly, aged forty, Roman Catholic, cooper, father of five children, married to Helen Donnelly, and Head of the Family at 26 St Ignatius Road, Drumcondra.*

What must his life have been like? wondered Garrett. What were his hopes and fears? And could he ever have imagined that one day, almost one hundred and ten years later, his great-great-grandson would be reading his census entry?

Garrett looked at the form again. He wasn't sure what a cooper was. In fact, before today, he didn't even know his great-great-grandfather's name. But he liked the idea of Thomas Donnelly living in Drumcondra, through which the Royal Canal flowed. Garrett could actually see the sparkling waters of the Ashtown stretch of the canal from his bedroom window, and he wondered if Thomas once swam in or walked along the canal, as Garrett liked to do all these years later.

Garrett looked at the dates again and did some mental arithmetic. Garrett's father, a civil servant in the Department of Finance, claimed that kids today couldn't do mental arithmetic because they were so dependent on electronic calculating. Garrett knew there was some truth in this, but he liked maths, and he liked even better to prove Dad wrong by being quick with his own mental calculations. Doing his sums now, he reasoned that if Thomas Donnelly had lived to be seventy-five – a good age back then – he would have died in 1946. But Garrett's grandmother was eighty-one, so according to his calculations their lives might have briefly overlapped.

One way to find out, he thought excitedly. Each Wednesday afternoon Granny came for dinner, and right now she was downstairs in the kitchen with Mam.

Garrett rose quickly from the desk, exited his bedroom and descended the stairs. He entered the kitchen, his appetite suddenly whetted by the smell of the roast chicken that was cooking in the oven.

'Garrett,' cried his grandmother mischievously, 'you've emerged from the Batcave!'

'Someone's got to protect Gotham City, Granny,' he retorted with a grin. 'Where's Mam?'

'In the utility room, putting on a wash.'

'Right.'

'Finished your homework?'

'It wasn't actually tonight's homework I was doing. It's a project.'

'Ah.'

Garrett sat beside his grandmother at the table. 'And you might be able to help me with it.'

'Me?'

'Our class are doing projects on our family trees. So I wondered if you remember your grandfather, Thomas Donnelly?'

Granny looked serious, and hesitated briefly before nodding. 'Yes. But he died when I was a little girl. So I remember very little of him.'

'Do you know where he was born, or where he grew up?'

'No. Sorry, Garrett.'

'And what about his wife – your grandmother?'

'She died when I was five. I barely remember her.'

'Right. And would you know where she was born?'

'I'm…I'm not sure where she came from,' said Granny. 'Sure isn't it enough to have gone back as far as you have?'

'Well, yes, but it would be great to go back even further. Did you ever hear either of them talking about their parents?'

Granny shook her head decisively. 'No, I didn't. Anyway, they're all long since dead. Best to just say a prayer for their souls and let them rest in peace.'

Before Garrett could respond his mother came back into the kitchen.

'Good man, Garrett,' she said, 'smell of food bring you down?'

'No.'

'I believe you – but thousands wouldn't! Set the table there, will you?'

'OK.'

Granny and his mother began chatting about Granny's new slow cooker, and Garrett started to set the table, his thoughts slightly unsettled. Something about Granny's response had struck a wrong note. Normally she was supportive about everything he did. So why was she dismissive of his efforts to explore the family tree? *Best to say a prayer and let the dead rest in peace?* He wouldn't push her on it for now, but something told him that there was a story here, and he wondered what on earth it might be.

CHAPTER THREE

Ballydowd, County Westmeath

SATURDAY 9th OCTOBER 1880

Molly felt anxious as she tried to get up the nerve to question her father. The family had finished dinner, and now Da was relaxing in the living room of their home adjoining the Royal Irish Constabulary station in the centre of the village. Da had taken his boots off and raised his feet onto a stool, and he was puffing contentedly on his sweet-smelling pipe.

Molly hesitated, trying to find the right words. Knowing Da's busy schedule, she mightn't get a chance like this for some time, with her mother tidying up in the kitchen, and her little sister Helen playing with her dolls in the bedroom. Molly's two older brothers were away from home, with twenty-year-old Frank serving with the British Army in India, and eighteen-year-old Mick following in Da's footsteps and away training at the police depot in Dublin.

Now was the moment, Molly knew. She sat quietly in the corner, a book in her hand, as she tried to decide exactly what she should say. Before she could speak, however, Da cocked his head and looked at her.

'Everything all right, love?'

Molly realised that her worry must have shown, and that her father, an experienced policeman, had read her body language.

'I eh…I just wanted to ask you something,' she said, closing the book.

'Ask away,' said Da. He took his pipe from his mouth and smiled encouragingly. 'I won't bite you.'

Molly tried for a smile in return. 'I wanted…I wanted to ask you about your job.'

Her father looked a little surprised. 'Yes? What did you want to know?'

'Well…people are…people are saying that the Royal Irish Constabulary are on the wrong side – in all this trouble with the Land League.'

'What people?'

Molly didn't want to name names so she shrugged. 'Just…other children in school and in the village.'

'Are they picking on you?' asked Da, lowering his feet from the stool and looking enquiringly at Molly.

'Not exactly. But I feel a bit uncomfortable sometimes. Having you as our local sergeant – it used to be good, people respected us. But now…'

'Now the Land League are poisoning the atmosphere.'

Molly didn't want to contradict her father, but she thought this was only half the story. The Land League's efforts to get basic rights for poor tenant farmers was a good idea, she believed, even if their methods were sometimes wrong. 'I know some Land League people are breaking the law,' she said.

Da drew on his pipe, and looked her in the eye. 'I'm waiting for the "but".'

'But they're saying that evicted families are left sleeping rough in fields or barns, or living like beggars in the workhouse. And people are saying the RIC are bullyboys for the landlords. That the police are too violent at evictions. I'm…I'm not sure what to say back to them.'

Her father didn't reply for a moment, and when he spoke his tone was gentle. 'Have I ever raised my hand to you, Molly?'

'No.'

'Have you ever seen me mistreat Mick, or Frank, or Helen, or your mam?'

'No, Da.'

'That's because I'm not a bullyboy.'

'I didn't mean you, Da!'

'Most of the men I work with aren't bullyboys either.'

'But…are some of them? Are some more violent than they

should be?'

Her father shrugged. 'We're not perfect. But we're up against thugs and criminals.'

'But, Da, aren't most people in the Land League just ordinary farmers? You can understand them not wanting to be evicted.'

'I can. But if the law says someone's to be evicted, we've no choice. The government makes the law, not the RIC. It's our job then to carry it out, whether we like it or not.'

'And…and what about the policemen who go too far?'

'What about the Land League thugs who go too far? Who maim cattle and threaten people?'

'They shouldn't,' said Molly. 'But…I suppose people expect the police to behave better than that.'

'And we generally do. But it's an imperfect world, Molly. At times like this we have to choose sides. Our family's done well out of the RIC. So for better or worse, that's the side we're on.'

'Right.'

'I can have a word though, if someone is giving you a hard time.'

'No, it's OK, Da.'

'Sure?'

'Yes, I just wanted to ask you about it.'

'You were right to. So next time someone talks about the RIC, you ask them right back about Land League outrages.'

Molly thought that that sounded fine at home. She suspected though that in the schoolyard or on the streets of the village it might not work so well. She didn't say so to her father, however, and instead she nodded.

'Nothing else bothering you?'

'No, Da.'

'Good girl.'

Her father went back to drawing on his pipe, and Molly gave him what she hoped was a reassuring smile, even though she knew, deep down, that there could be trouble ahead.

Clara heard a loud crack of thunder, then a moment later she saw a flash of lightning through the large Georgian windows of the dining room of Parkinson House. Clara normally loved to watch lightning with her nose pressed to the windowpane, but tonight she stayed at the table politely eating.

She felt happy as she slipped the last mouthful of apple tart into her mouth. It was one of her favourite desserts, and a dish that Cook did to perfection, with just the right mixture of tangy apples and soft, sugar-sweetened pastry. Clara's pleasure, however, didn't stem from the meal alone; she was pleased too with what had been an eventful day. She felt no ill-effects from her fall in the woods and had managed to return Kaiser to the stables uninjured. She was also intrigued by her encounter with Aidan and was excited by the idea of their secret rendezvous to go fishing tomorrow afternoon.

Her mother and father had returned from their trip to the Belvedere estate outside Mullingar, and Clara had joined them, along with her Aunt Esther, after everyone had dressed for dinner. At twenty-six years of age Aunt Esther was the baby sister of Clara's father William, and Clara enjoyed the company of her youthful aunt. Esther was to be married in the spring, and Clara had savoured the excitement of her engagement and was already looking forward to next year's wedding.

Now, however, the mood at the dining table had taken a serious turn as Esther asked how the trip to Belvedere had gone.

'Very pleasant lunch,' said Clara's mother, 'but marred by news from Mayo.'

'Really?' said Esther, who always liked to hear the latest gossip.

Clara could sense though that the news her mother referred to was something serious.

'It's the Land League,' she continued, 'they're making life impossible for landowners.'

'What are they doing now, Mama?' asked Clara.

Her mother hesitated and glanced at her husband.

'She may as well hear it from us, Florence, she'll hear it anyway,' he said, before turning to Clara. 'They're damaging landlords' property, they're harming animals, and they're destroying crops.'

'That's awful,' said Clara.

'Yes, it is. And now they've gone further.'

'How?' asked Esther.

'They're trying to ruin Captain Boycott, Lord Erne's land agent. The local people won't harvest his crops, his servants have abandoned him, and no one will cook his meals or wash his clothes. The local shops in Ballinrobe won't supply him with food. It's appalling.'

'Why are they so angry with him, Papa?'

'They're in dispute about rents and evictions.'

'Mind you, I have heard that Charles Boycott is not the easiest man to get on with,' said Esther.

'Be that as it may, they don't have the right to ruin a man.'

Even though Clara could see her father's point, it seemed to her that what was being done to Captain Boycott wasn't as awful as being evicted onto the side of the road. The thunder and lightning had brought with it a downpour of heavy rain, and Clara thought how miserable it must be tonight for those people who had lost their homes. She didn't want to seem disloyal to her own family, however, so she said nothing.

'And what are the Royal Irish Constabulary doing about it all?' asked Esther.

'Not half enough,' said her sister-in-law.

'Well, it's difficult,' conceded Clara's father. 'Anyone caught damaging property or crops is arrested. But the other behaviour isn't actually illegal. It's despicable and cowardly, but if people shun you, if the blacksmith won't shoe your horse or the shopkeeper won't sell you groceries, they're not breaking any law.'

'Captain Boycott actually had to have food taken in from Cong by boat,' said Clara's mother.

'Really?' said Esther. 'You would have thought some local

people would be glad to have his business.'

'Of course they would. But they're intimidated not to. It's pure blackguardism.'

Clara was a little taken aback by her father's words. Normally Papa was moderate in his views, and she knew that the Parkinsons had traditionally been regarded as good landlords who got on well with their tenants.

'If someone refuses to ostracise whoever is being sent to Coventry, then *they themselves* get ostracised,' continued her father, 'that's what allows it to infect a whole community.'

'It sounds like the Land League has come up with a very effective weapon,' said Esther. 'And if it works against Charles Boycott…'

'It could quickly spread to other disputes. Which would be disastrous,' said Clara's mother.

For Mama to become agitated by politics was unusual, and Clara felt a flutter of unease. Before she knew what she was doing she blurted out her fear. 'Does that mean…could people do that to us? Refuse to pick our crops or sell us food or anything?'

'No. No, I think that's most unlikely, Clara,' said her father reassuringly. 'We've always played fair with our tenants. When harvests were bad we accepted lower rents. So don't worry yourself. What's happening in Mayo won't happen in Ballydowd. All right?'

'All right, Papa,' answered Clara, relieved by his soothing words. And yet, a small seed of unease had been planted in her mind. Ballydowd was a long way from the upheaval going on in county

Mayo, but the Land League was growing in power, and who knew what the future might bring? Clara knew from listening to her parents that the government had set up a commission, headed by Lord Bessborough, to hear evidence from tenant farmers, landlords and agents. The commission was holding dozens of sittings to examine rent, tenant security, and land ownership, and the commission's recommendations – which could change things dramatically – were due in a few more months.

Well, she would worry about all of that when the time came. For now she was hoping that the heavy rain wouldn't last long, and that she could meet Aidan for their fishing trip tomorrow. Excited by the thought of their secret rendezvous, she leaned forward and helped herself to another portion of apple tart.

CHAPTER FOUR

'I've a good one for you, Molly,' said Aidan with a grin.

'Go on then.'

'What do you call a horse that lives next door?'

'What?' she asked, a smile forming on her lips even before Aidan gave the answer.

'A *neigh*-bour!'

Molly laughed, then playfully pointed at her friend. 'I've one for you. Why was the dog a bad dancer?'

'Why?'

'Because he had two left feet!'

Aidan laughed and he was glad that he had met Molly after Sunday morning Mass. Last night's thunder and lightning had given way to a mild autumn morning, and the main street of Bal-lydowd was bathed in hazy October sunshine as they walked in the direction of her home. Aidan had known Molly O'Hara since they had started in school together as four-year-olds, and now, eight years later, they were good friends.

It made him feel a little guilty when Molly asked him what he was doing this afternoon. He answered that he was going fish-ing – but made no mention of Clara Parkinson. He knew that Molly was going with her father into Mullingar, the nearest big town, and that he wouldn't have seen her this afternoon anyhow.

But not mentioning Clara Parkinson somehow felt dishonest. On the other hand he had agreed with Clara that it was to be a secret meeting. And if something happened, and Clara couldn't get away, or if she had second thoughts and didn't show up, then he didn't want to look stupid in Molly's eyes. *Better to say nothing, and see how things go this afternoon,* he decided.

'Bye, Aidan,' said Molly, as they came to a halt outside the RIC station. 'Enjoy your fishing.'

'Thanks. Enjoy Mullingar.'

'See you in school tomorrow.'

'Thanks for reminding me!' said Aidan, then he waved in farewell and set off down the street. There was something about Sunday mornings that he really liked. Part of it was not having to attend school, and the fact that the family always had a nicer dinner on Sundays. But part of it was the sense of occasion. Whether attending Mass in the Catholic chapel, or Sunday service in the Anglican Church, people dressed in their best clothes. Aidan himself was in his good trousers and jacket and, although he would have to change out of them as soon as he came home from Mass, he liked looking smart. The other local boys weren't very interested in clothes, but Aidan was intrigued by design and the way fashions changed. He knew his father wanted him to follow in his footsteps and be a farmer. Aidan, though, had never had the nerve to tell Da that his real dream was to work in a big department store, advising customers on fabrics and fashions, and maybe even running his own shop one day.

No point having that conversation until he had to, he had decided, and meanwhile he was happy enough to help out on the family farm. Though of course it wasn't *really* the Daly's farm, in that they were tenant farmers whose thirty-five-acre holding was actually owned by an absentee landlord. Many of the other small farms in the area were tenants of the Parkinson estate, and Aidan thought how unlikely it would have seemed just a day ago that he would soon be meeting the daughter of the man who held so much power over the lives of the people of Ballydowd. Then again, maybe that power would be lessened if things in Mayo were anything to go by. It was an interesting time to be growing up in Ireland he reckoned. Then he dismissed all thoughts of politics, and walked on through the autumn sunshine, looking forward to his Sunday dinner and his secret meeting.

'The time for talking is over,' said Sean Kearney. 'It's time for action.'

'Careful, Sean.'

'No, Larry! We've been careful too long.'

Aidan listened, fascinated, as his father and his Uncle Sean spoke in low tones in the quiet of the barn. Aidan hadn't intended to spy on them. He had slipped into the gloomy barn to get his fishing gear, but something about the two men's secretive demeanour as they approached the building had caused him to step back into the shadows. Now Aidan couldn't reveal himself without having to explain why he had been eavesdropping, and instead he stood stock-still.

Besides, he was intrigued by the conversation. Uncle Sean, Mam's hot-headed brother, was a bachelor and a small farmer who lived in a ramshackle cottage about halfway between Ballydowd and Mullingar. He worked hard to earn a modest living and had enthusiastically taken up the cause when the Land League began organising the small farmers and labourers. Aidan's father had also joined the League, but Da had always been less impulsive than Uncle Sean.

'We've *always* been careful,' said Sean. 'Respecting our so-called betters. *Yes, sir, no sir, three bags full, sir. Evict us onto the side of the road if you want to, sir!*'

'I take your point,' said Da, 'but we need to pick our battles. The landlords have money and power – and they've got the RIC, and the army to back them up. I'm just saying we need to be smart in how we act.'

'But now we have them rattled. We were never this organised before.'

Aidan knew that Mr Parnell, who was a member of parliament in Westminster, and the Leader of the Irish Parliamentary Party, had joined forces with Michael Davitt, the leader of the Land League, to organise the fight for basic rights for Irish farmers.

'We've frightened the landlords,' said Sean. 'But if all we do is talk, they won't stay frightened for long.'

'So what are you saying?'

'We're winning the battle in Mayo because everyone is standing together against Boycott. That didn't happen by accident.'

Aidan could tell that his father wasn't comfortable. 'Are you saying people were threatened, to make them toe the line?' he asked.

'Of course they were!' said Sean with exasperation. 'This is a war, Larry. Like you just said, they've got the money, and the police, and the army. We've got to use whatever weapons we have. We've got to get our hands dirty.'

'I'll never agree to maiming cattle or shooting people who don't agree with us,' said Da.

'It's the last thing I want either,' said Sean. 'But if they try to evict a family onto the side of the road we can't just stand by – and they're planning to do that to the Horans the week after next. If we let them evict the Horans today, it could be you or me on the side of the road tomorrow.'

'I know,' said Da uneasily.

Aidan thought of the long hours that his father worked, and it seemed horribly unfair that even if you worked hard and paid your rent, you could still be thrown out of your home on the whim of a landlord.

'If there's trouble we won't be the ones to start it,' continued Sean. 'But by God we won't walk away from it either. The Land League in Mayo sent a message to the Boycotts of this world. Here in Westmeath we need to do the same. And the way we do it is by every man, woman, and child in this area standing united. All right?'

'All right,' answered Da, 'but now I need to get back.'

Aidan stood unmoving as the two men left the barn, *Every man, woman and child*, Uncle Sean said. So Aidan too would be expected to play a part. He had only just met Clara Parkinson, and yet, already, it seemed like the world was conspiring to prevent them from becoming friends.

CHAPTER FIVE

Ashtown, Dublin 15

FRIDAY 21st FEBRUARY 2020

Garrett heard the ping of a message on his mobile phone, but he resisted the temptation to look at the device. *You don't have to respond to a message at once* was one of his father's catch phrases. And although reluctant to admit it, he could actually see Dad's point, even though it was hard to ignore the attention-catching beep. Today, though, Garrett was so engrossed that he had no difficulty holding off on checking his phone.

He was sitting at the desk in the cosy warmth of his bedroom, writing the details of his family tree onto a large cardboard chart, and his head was filled with thoughts of the past. He had gone back over the generations in both his mother's and his father's families, and he realised that his ancestors had lived through turbulent times in Irish history. They had experienced the First World

War, the Easter Rising, the War of Independence, the Civil War, and more recent generations had lived through the Second World War and the Troubles in Northern Ireland.

Garrett loved computers, and coding, and technology in general, but there was something enjoyably old-school about hand-writing the details into the family-tree chart that he had bought in the local bookshop. But while the layout of the chart enabled him to get an overview of marriages, births and deaths among his ancestors, he had become really curious about the details of their daily lives. *What songs had they sung, where did they attend school, what books did they read, where did they go on holidays?* He had questioned Mam and Dad about their childhood memories, and what they had heard from their parents about the past.

Between studying online census forms, talking to his parents, and looking at old photographs, Garrett was building up a fascinating portrait of the extended family, with details about jobs, reading and writing ability, height and weight, and even hair colour. Garrett's own red hair had won him the nickname 'Ginger' in school, and he had been pleased to hear from his father that Granddad, whom Garrett just barely remembered, also had red hair when he was young. Dad didn't know if Granddad had been called Ginger when he was a boy, but Garrett hoped that he had. Even if he hadn't, Garrett felt that the family-tree project had established a tiny link between him and his dead grandfather, and the notion pleased him.

On both sides of the family he had gone back over one hundred years. But Granny, his mother's mother, was the only one of his four grandparents still alive, so the living memories stopped with her. Thinking of Granny, Garrett put down his pen and gazed distractedly out the bedroom window. His mind went back to the conversation earlier in the week. Was it really credible that his grandmother – so alert and curious in every other respect – knew so little about her grandparents? Or was she hiding something? And if she was, what could it be that still mattered after all these years?

Then again, maybe he was making a mountain out of a mole-hill. He enjoyed puzzles and the solving of mysteries, and perhaps he was creating a mystery where none existed. After all, what had Granny actually done? Hesitated when asked about the past, and suggested letting the dead rest in peace? Was that really so unusual in a woman of eighty-one?

But still. There had been something in her manner that hadn't quite rung true. He sat gazing out the window, then made his mind up. *He had to take it further.* He wouldn't hound Granny, and would come at the problem sideways, but if there was a mystery in the past he was determined to solve it. Pleased with his decision, he swung round in the chair, picked up his pen, and resumed writing up the details of his family tree.

CHAPTER SIX

Clara thought how unpredictable life could be. Even a day ago what she was doing now would have seemed highly unlikely, yet here she was, fishing off a fallen log on the bank of the river, enjoying the sounds of birdsong and the gentle burbling of the water as it swirled over protruding rocks. The river sparkled in the October sunshine, the air had the tang of autumn, and Clara was glad she had held her nerve and kept her appointment to meet Aidan Daly.

She had been nervous all morning, wondering if she was being foolish in meeting a boy from one of the tenant farms at a time when tension was mounting between landlords and tenants. There had also been the possibility that Aidan would have second thoughts and not show up, or that her mother or father would create some last-minute difficulty that would prevent her from getting away. She had sat through Sunday School this morning barely taking in a word that was said, and she had been a little distracted too when the family had Sunday lunch.

All her worries had turned out to be in vain, however. After changing out of her Sunday clothes of tailored overcoat, hat, and gloves, she had slipped into a more practical pinafore and jacket, claiming she was going for a walk, and had met up with Aidan at the arranged spot by the river. They had been a little shy as he handed her a spare fishing rod, but the slight awkwardness of suddenly finding themselves together again soon eased, and within minutes they had resumed the relaxed relationship of yesterday.

They had walked westwards along the riverbank, in the opposite direction to Ballydowd, until they came to a secluded spot that Aidan said was one of the best places for catching fish. He had baited a line for her and shown her how to cast, and now they sat companionably on the fallen log, each with a rod in hand.

'How did you learn to fish?' asked Clara.

'My Uncle Sean taught me.'

'Does he live with you?'

'No, he lives about five miles away.'

'My Aunt Esther lives with us. But…'

'She thinks young ladies shouldn't fish,' interjected Aidan playfully.

Clara smiled. 'She probably does. Though she's not a stick-in-the-mud. Just…just a bit sensible about some things.'

'Right.'

'But I really like her. I suppose if your uncle taught you to fish, you like him too?'

'Yes. Though no one would ever say Uncle Sean is too sensible.'

'Why, is he impulsive?'

Aidan hesitated briefly, then nodded. 'He can be sometimes,' he answered carefully. 'So, what's it like to a have a governess instead of going to school?'

Clara sensed that the subject was being deliberately changed, but something told her not to press the matter of Aidan's uncle. Instead she shrugged. 'It's all right. She's nice enough. I can't really say if it's better than school, because the only school I've gone to is Sunday School.'

'And do you like that?' asked Aidan.

Clara suspected that being a Catholic – like most people were in Ballydowd – Aidan was curious about the Protestant religion of the gentry, and she answered his question honestly. 'I like meeting the other boys and girls at Sunday School. But I don't like listening to the vicar rambling on about Old Testament prophets.'

'It could be worse,' said Aidan with a grin. 'You could have to listen to Father Vaughan going on about sinners.'

'Oh?'

'*They'll roast on the hottest hob of Hell with their tongues hanging out!*' exclaimed Aidan, putting on an angry, elderly voice.

Clara burst out laughing. Normally when it came to Catholics and Protestants talking about their faiths each group tended to be careful about what they said, and Clara found it refreshing that Aidan was good-humouredly irreverent. 'You're good at accents,' she said.

'Not as good as my sister Maud. She used to be able to listen to someone for ten seconds and take them off perfectly.'

'Used to? Has she stopped?'

'Knowing Maud, probably not. But she got married to a farmer from Roscommon, so she lives there now.'

'And have you other brothers or sisters?'

42

'I've three more sisters, Theresa, Peg and Brigid. I'm the baby of the family, and the girls always say I'm the pet!'

Clara had never before had a conversation like this with someone from the village and she realised how little she knew of the daily lives of her father's tenants. 'And your sisters – what do they do? If I'm not being too nosy,' she added hastily, hoping that her curiosity wouldn't seem rude.

'No,' said Aidan, 'it's no big secret. Theresa works in a mill in England, in Bradford. Peg is a housemaid for a family up in Dublin, and Brigid helps on the farm, but she's been promised a start in a shop in Galway after Christmas.'

Clara was glad that Aidan's family seemed to be making their way in the world, even if it was sad that all of them had to leave their home in Ballydowd.

'And what about your family?' he asked.

'Mama is originally from Norfolk. Her father was a bishop there, and she met my father when he was an officer in the army. Aunt Esther is Papa's sister. She'll be leaving us next year to marry a doctor who's away at the moment with his regiment in Calcutta. And I'm an only child.' On impulse Clara decided to be as open as Aidan, and she smiled. 'A spoiled brat is how I overheard one of the girls in Sunday School describe me!'

'I'm sure that's not true.'

'Well, I probably do get my own way a bit. And I'm more the centre of attention than if I had brothers or sisters,' she conceded.

'And would you like to have had a brother or sister?'

Nobody had ever asked Clara this before, and she had to consider for a moment. 'I've never known anything else, so I'm happy enough. But sometimes it's a bit lonely, and it would be nice to have company.'

Aidan seemed thoughtful, then he looked at her enquiringly. 'Do you play any musical instrument?' he asked.

Clara was taken aback by the question. 'Eh, yes,' she answered, 'the violin and the piano. Why?'

'My friend Molly and I get together,' said Aidan. 'She's great on the melodeon, and I play the tin whistle. You could play with us sometimes, if you like.'

Clara was touched by the spontaneous way that Aidan was open to sharing, whether it was his knowledge of fishing or the opportunity to play music. 'That…that would be very nice, thank you.' she answered. 'But…well, wouldn't some people frown at us all mixing?'

Aidan grinned. 'As you said yourself – only if they knew. And Molly would enjoy secret music sessions.'

'You think so?'

'I've known her all my life. I guarantee it.'

'Right,' said Clara. 'And what sort of music do you play?'

'Anything that takes our fancy. Traditional airs, Percy French tunes, there's a new song called *Polly Wolly Doodle* that we've learnt. What do you play?'

'Mostly classical, some of the Gilbert and Sullivan songs. The latest piece I've learnt is *Brahms's Waltz in A Major.*'

44

Aidan laughed. 'Our latest piece is *Shoe the Donkey*. Bit of a difference.'

Clara hoped that she hadn't sounded snooty in her music choices. 'I wasn't trying to sound high-falutin',' she said. 'It's just, they're the pieces I've been taught.'

'You're grand. Sure at the end of the day it's all music.'

Clara felt relieved at Aidan's easy-going approach. She knew, though, that her parents wouldn't be quite so easy-going, and that they would say it was inappropriate for her to mix with children of a different class. She didn't like going behind their backs, but after only twenty-four hours she sensed already that Aidan would make a good friend. Well, *nothing ventured, nothing gained,* as Aunt Esther often said. 'I'd love to play music with you and Molly,' she said. 'When do you next meet up?'

'We don't have a special time. But I'll talk to her tomorrow and then...' Aidan never finished the sentence, however. Instead he was interrupted by a cry from Clara.

'I think I've a fish!' she cried. 'I think I've a fish on my line! What do I do?'

'Don't panic,' said Aidan. 'I'll guide you through it, OK?'

'OK,' answered Clara excitedly. 'OK!'

The sun was dipping in the sky, bathing the riverbank in a golden glow, and Aidan wished that the afternoon didn't have to end.

The time with Clara Parkinson had passed quickly, and he had been fascinated by the insight Clara provided into life in Parkinson House, from the food they ate to the differing uniforms that the staff wore. For someone used to the luxury of a household serviced by a large team of servants and gardeners, she was surprisingly down-to-earth.

Aidan had enjoyed too the experience of seeing angling afresh, through the eyes of a beginner, and he had shared Clara's excitement at catching her first trout. She couldn't bring it home, as their afternoon together had to remain secret, but the obvious pleasure she got from going fishing made the subterfuge worthwhile.

Now, however, she turned to him in alarm. 'Aidan! I think someone's coming.'

Aidan strained his ears and heard a rustling noise, the faint drone of approaching voices. So far he and Clara had been uninterrupted at the remote riverside location, but they had allowed for this possibility, and he quickly gathered his rod and bag and retreated into the thick bushes that flanked the river.

Aidan listened intently as the voices drew nearer. He peeked carefully through a small gap in the bushes, standing stock still so as to remain invisible to whoever was drawing nearer. After a moment he recognised the speakers and his heart sank. It was the Tobin twins, Peadar and Iggy, two local boys of his own age that Aidan had never liked. They were stockily built and cocky, and when the mood took them they bullied those weaker than themselves.

Aidan hoped they wouldn't pick on Clara when they saw her here alone. If they did, he would have to intervene, but then they would know that he and Clara had been meeting, and that would bring its own problems.

He watched as they spotted Clara and exchanged a glance. Aidan was impressed by Clara's coolness in continuing to fish without looking around at the approaching boys. But would she stay calm if the Tobins ganged up on her?

'What have we got here' said Peadar in a sing-song, mocking tone.

'What are you doin'?' asked Iggy drawing nearer to Clara.

Still seated on the fallen log, she turned around and looked him in the eye. 'I'm fishing, obviously,' she answered.

Aidan could see from the twins' faces that they recognised her and were surprised to find the daughter of the Big House out here alone. Aidan swallowed hard, aware that Clara didn't know the personality of the twins, and that things could quickly spiral out of control if they felt she was making little of them. On the other hand to cross a family as powerful as the Parkinsons was a big step to take, and Aidan hoped that even boys as dim-witted as the Tobins would realise that.

'You're a long way from home, aren't you?' said Peadar, moving closer to Clara.

'So?'

'So, anything could happen out here...' said Iggy.

There was a definite undercurrent of menace in Iggy's words, and Aidan knew they wanted to frighten her. Or maybe worse. He steeled himself to act if need be. Taking on the Tobin twins was a daunting prospect, but he couldn't stay in hiding if they mistreated Clara.

For a moment she said nothing, then, to Aidan's surprise, she lowered her fishing rod, rose, and walked right up to Iggy.

'That almost sounded like a threat,' she said quietly. 'For your sake, I hope I took it up wrong. Did I?'

Aidan was gobsmacked by her coolness. Although he could imagine how a life of privilege would give someone like Clara a sense of confidence, he hadn't expected this. Iggy was clearly taken by surprise too and seemed uncertain how to react. Aidan bit his lip, knowing that this could still end badly.

Clara switched her gaze to Peadar. 'Cat got your tongue as well?' she asked.

Aidan sensed that Peadar was unsure whether to back down or not, but as he hesitated, Clara spoke again.

'I'm going to do you boys a favour. I'm going to assume you meant no harm. The wise thing now would be to take advantage of that, and be on your way.'

Aidan held his breath. The Tobins *weren't* wise, and they might still do something stupid to salvage their pride. Nobody moved for a moment, then Peadar acted. Reaching out his hand he clapped his brother on the shoulder.

'Come on, Igg,' he said, in an obvious attempt to sound casual. 'We've better things to do than standing here talking tripe.'

Iggy looked relieved to have the decision taken out of his hands. 'Dead right,' he said, then he followed his brother, trying to disguise their retreat by walking away with an exaggerated swagger.

Aidan felt like cheering. He loved how Clara had handled the bullies, but secrecy was still vital, so he waited till he was certain that the Tobins were well gone before stepping out on the riverbank.

'You were brilliant,' he said.

'I was, wasn't I?' she said, then laughed.

Aidan laughed too, and in that moment he sensed that whatever problems the future brought, he and Clara were definitely going to be friends.

CHAPTER SEVEN

Molly felt a little sad, though she tried not to show it. Until recently she had taken for granted that people liked her, and she had got on well with her school mates and most people in the village. She was a regular winner at running and jumping in the annual Ballydowd Sports Day, and the combination of being outgoing and athletic had made her popular. Now, however, the mood had changed, and although she wouldn't admit it to her father, she wished sometimes that she wasn't a policeman's daughter.

She was in her draughty classroom in Ballydowd National School, and was now the only O'Hara on the roll book, with her little sister Helen not due to start school until next September. Mr Quigley had left the room for a few moments and had given his usual warning that there would be skin and hair flying if he came back to an unruly classroom. The pupils knew though that their kindly teacher was unlikely to punish them, and chatter had broken out once he had gone.

The Tobin twins sat together in the desk behind Molly, and Iggy Tobin had started talking disparagingly about the RIC. Molly knew he was doing it to make her uncomfortable, and it was disappointing when other pupils laughed at Iggy's mocking tone. Molly realised that many of her classmates didn't particularly like the Tobins, and that some of them were laughing along so as not to cross Iggy. It still hurt, though, to be made feel an outsider in a place where she had always felt she belonged. Even Aidan had seemed slightly different when she had spoken with him before class this morning, and she hoped that her oldest friend wouldn't start keeping his distance now that the RIC were becoming unpopular because of the Land War.

Peadar Tobin was going on about well-fed policemen picking on poor farmers who had barely enough to eat. Neither Iggy nor Peadar had ever shown much concern for anyone but themselves, and Molly felt her anger growing, knowing the Tobins were just using the topic to get at her.

'I often wonder, Iggy,' said Peadar with mock sincerity. 'How do those coppers sleep at night?'

'Good question, Peadar.'

Molly felt her patience snap and she turned around in her desk. 'Actually, it's a stupid question. They lie down and close their eyes like everyone else. But if you've something to say about my father, why don't you just come out and say it?!'

'Fine!' said Iggy, moving his face aggressively towards Molly. 'I will then. Your father is RIC, and they're doing the landlords' dirty work. So tell us, how does he sleep at night?'

Before Molly could respond, Peadar raised his hand as though answering a question in class.

'I think I know,' he said. 'I'd say Molly sings him to sleep – with 'God Save the Queen'! Several of the other pupils laughed, and

Molly wasn't sure how to respond. Before she could think up an answer, Aidan also raised his hand. Molly had felt bad that some of her classmates had laughed at the 'God Save the Queen' jibe. But the ones who had laughed weren't her friends, whereas Aidan was. If he made fun of her it would really feel like a betrayal. Up until now the fact that Aidan's family was pro-Land League hadn't caused a problem between them, but now Molly wasn't sure where she stood.

'Talking of singing,' said Aidan. 'What has forty feet and sings?'

'What?' asked Iggy.

'The school choir!' answered Aidan.

Several of the children laughed, and Molly could see that Iggy was annoyed at Aidan for changing the subject.

'Why did the singer climb a ladder?' continued Aidan, before immediately giving the answer 'He wanted to reach the high notes'!

It was a silly joke, but again people laughed. Molly felt a surge of affection for her friend, along with a touch of guilt for ever having doubted him. It was clear that Aidan had intervened to stop the Tobins from picking on her, but by doing it humorously it was hard for the twins to object.

Molly could see that Peadar and Iggy were uncertain how to react, and she turned her back on them, hoping that would end the confrontation. Just then Mr Quigley returned to the class room.

'Aren't ye the right pack of heartscalds?' he said, 'Kicking up a rumpus the minute my back is turned! Take out your English readers, and not another peep out of you.'

Molly reached into her schoolbag, relieved by the teacher's return. Despite his colourful turn of phrase he wasn't really angry with his pupils, and now that he was back in the classroom the incident with the Tobins could be left behind. She knew, however, that it was only a temporary reprieve and that life as a policeman's daughter wasn't going to get easier. But for now the Tobins had been contained, and Aidan was still her friend. She gave him a quick wink, opened her English reader and sat back in her desk.

The school bell rang for midday break, and there was a flurry of activity as the pupils scampered for the classroom door. Aidan was a little uneasy, but he knew he could no longer put off the conversation he needed to have with Molly.

'Can we…can we talk for a minute?' he said to her as they made for the school yard. Aidan and Molly both lived within walking distance of the school and they usually went home with other children for dinner during the break. Today though, he wanted to talk to her in private, and she stopped and looked at him enquiringly.

'That sounds serious.'

'Well, it kind of is,' he answered.

'We'll follow you on,' called Molly to the other pupils who were heading for home, then she turned back to Aidan. There was a scent of burning leaves in the autumn air, but the day was warm, and Aidan indicated a bench in the corner of the school yard, away from where some of the younger children were playing chasing.

'Let's head over there.' he suggested.

They moved to the bench and sat, then Molly looked at him enquiringly. 'What's wrong?'

Aidan hesitated a moment, then looked his friend in the eye. 'I eh…I didn't tell you the whole truth yesterday.'

'About what?'

'About going fishing. I…I didn't go on my own.'

'Who did you go with?'

'I went…I went with Clara Parkinson.'

'What?!'

'I feel bad for not telling you the truth, Molly. But I didn't want to sound stupid if I said I was meeting her, and then she didn't show up.'

'How did you get to know Clara Parkinson?'

'I was in the woods on Saturday, and she got thrown off her father's horse. She took a bad tumble, and I helped her up, and we got chatting.'

'And a day later you're fishing pals?'

'She'd never gone fishing in her life. And I'd been fishing that day. So she asked me would I show her how.'

'She never mixes with people like us. She must have taken a big shine to you.'

'Please, Molly…'

'What?'

'Don't be jealous. You're my best friend and you always will be. But I felt sorry for her. She sounded like her life is a bit lonely. And she likes music, so I…'

'You what?'

'I asked her if she'd like to play with us.'

'Did you now?'

Seeing Molly's expression, Aidan raised his hands in a gesture of surrender. 'I'm sorry, I shouldn't have just assumed you'd agree. I don't blame you for being angry.'

Molly held his gaze for a moment. Then she seemed to reach a decision. 'I'm not angry with you, Aidan. You…you always want to do the right thing. Like you did with me and the Tobins this morning. So we're still best friends.'

'Thanks.'

'But you need to be careful. Mixing with Clara Parkinson could cause trouble.'

'You mean if people found out?'

'Yes. Can you imagine what Iggy and Peadar Tobin would say?'

'They'd go mad. But fooling people like them is part of the fun. We did the fishing in secret, and the three of us playing music could be a secret too. Clara's good fun, Molly, I know you'd like her.'

'Maybe. But her family probably think we're not good enough to be her friend.'

'And our families are probably just as set in their ways – in the opposite direction.'

'True,' conceded Molly.'

'Look, you and I are friends because we like each other, even though our families aren't friends. It can be the same with us and Clara.'

'And what about the Land League stuff? It's going to get — I don't know whether to say worse or better — but it's definitely heating up.'

'We need a break from all that. If we can secretly play music, and go fishing, and be friends, what's wrong with that?'

Molly looked thoughtful for a moment. 'Nothing, I suppose.'

'So are we on then?'

'OK.'

'Sure?'

'Yes, count me in.'

'Brilliant!' said Aidan happily. 'Brilliant!'

Clara sat up straight at the drawing room piano under the watchful eye of her governess, Miss Andrews. She played Chopin's Prelude Number 7, and although her mind wasn't fully on her playing, she was a sufficiently good pianist to keep Miss Andrews satisfied while she listened to the conversation between her mother and Aunt Esther, who were seated on an ornate sofa before a blazing log fire.

'I'm sorry, but once a servant is dismissed there's really no going back,' said her mother.

'It just seems a little harsh,' said Esther. 'She *is* a very pleasant girl.'

'Pleasant or unpleasant, I can't be seen to overrule Mr Harris. It would undermine his authority.'

Clara knew that they were talking about Mary O'Brien, a housemaid who had been sacked that morning, by the house steward, Mr Harris. The house steward was the most senior member of staff at Parkinson House and he had the power to hire and dismiss other servants.

'You couldn't suggest to Harris that he was entitled to punish Mary,' said Esther, 'but that a dressing down and a fine might suffice?'

Clara's mother responded in the gentle but unyielding tone that Clara recognised from when Mama felt obliged to take a stand.

'Your compassion does you credit, Esther,' she said. 'But Mary O'Brien knew the rules when she started here, and I can't intervene when the House Stewart implements those rules.'

Clara felt like saying that the rule was a stupid one. Mary had been sacked because she had a boyfriend – or a follower, as Mr Harris called it – and housemaids in Parkinson House were expected to concentrate on their jobs without the distraction of followers. Clara knew it would be no use arguing about it with her mother. As the daughter of a bishop Mama had always been obliged to follow the rules. It was something for which she was still a stickler, but Clara thought that once a housemaid did her job properly she should be entitled to see whoever she wanted in the limited free time that she was allowed.

Now Clara finished the Chopin piece with a flourish, and Miss Andrews nodded approvingly.

'Nicely played. If we can get your violin work up to the same standard, we'll be doing well.'

'Thank you,' said Clara, smiling wryly to herself and thinking that it was very governess-like to link a compliment with an exhortation to do better in some other field. But she liked Miss Andrews, a middle-aged Welsh woman whose prim demeanour masked a caring personality.

What would Miss Andrews think, though, if she knew that Clara had gone fishing with a boy from the village? In the five days since the fishing expedition Clara had thought a lot about Aidan Daly and their afternoon together. It had been exciting to catch her first fish, and Aidan had been good company. He had an impish sense of humour that made her laugh, and a curiosity about life in general, and in particular about her life as an only child in Parkinson House.

For her part Clara had been fascinated to get an insight into how things were for the families of the small farmers who were her father's tenants. She was thankful too that Aidan had suggested meeting up again, and even the confrontation with the Tobins had ended well and provided the afternoon with a dash of drama. Now the drawing room door opened, and Clara's musings were cut short by the arrival of her father.

'Papa!' she said in greeting.

'Clara,' he replied smilingly. 'All well on the music front, Miss Andrews?'

'Yes indeed. Note perfect on her Chopin.'

'Well done, Clara!'

Her mother and Aunt Esther greeted her father, and Clara sensed from his good spirits that his visit to Mullingar, the nearest big town, had gone well. She knew that he had been meeting some other landowners, and that the Land League would have been at the top of their agenda.

'Is something happening about Captain Boycott, Papa?' she asked.

'Come, come, Clara,' he answered. 'That's not something with which a young girl needs to concern herself.'

Clara felt a stab of irritation. He had spoken gently and didn't say it as a rebuke, but she resented being fobbed off as though she were a baby. She was twelve years old and next year she would be going to a boarding school – why shouldn't she want to know what was going on in the world around her? But she couldn't confront her father openly, and when he looked at her and said 'All right?' she nodded in reply.

'Yes, Papa.'

'I will say this, however,' continued her father, turning to his wife and sister. 'The Land League have been throwing their weight around, but they may find the tide turning. It's time to show them they don't run this country – we still do.'

'Hear, hear!' said Clara's mother.

'We'll discuss it later,' said Papa. 'Now if you'll excuse me, I'm going up to change.'

Clara wondered what had happened at the meeting in Mullingar. Clearly her father thought the Land League could be defeated, and he knew far more about politics than she did. And yet. As an only child with no siblings to guide her, Clara had learnt to trust her gut instincts. And her instinct was that if the landlords tried to wipe out the Land League there would be fierce resistance all over Ireland – including Ballydowd and the Parkinson estate. Troubled by the thought, she turned over her sheet music, drew nearer the piano, and tried to lose herself in the music.

CHAPTER EIGHT

Garrett felt a tingle go up his spine. He was sitting at the small desk in his bedroom, and he stared disbelievingly at an old black and white photograph. It had been mixed in with dozens of others in an envelope of family pictures that Dad had given him for the family-tree project. The picture had been taken professionally in a studio, and showed a slim, elegantly dressed man in his early thirties, seated beside his wife and two young children. Everyone in the photograph looked surprisingly serious, but what struck Garrett forcefully was the face of the man in the picture.

It was like looking into the future and seeing an older version of himself. The man had a moustache and was over twice the age of fourteen-year-old Garrett, but the resemblance was unmistakable. Garrett turned the picture over. Written in neat, faded handwriting were the words Raymond, Margaret, Damian, and Jane Byrne, Dublin, 1934.

Garrett realised that this was a family portrait of his father's grandparents with their children. Garrett had never before seen a picture of his great-grandfather and he couldn't get over the resemblance to himself. Garrett didn't look like his father or his deceased grandfather, but he had heard that sometimes genes could skip several generations, and clearly that had happened here.

Looking at the picture gave Garrett a weird sensation, as though he were time-travelling in two different directions at once. The Dublin of 1934 was over eighty years in the past, yet the appearance of Raymond Byrne was like a glimpse into how Garrett might look in the future. He picked up his mobile phone and took a picture of the photograph, knowing his friends in school would be entertained by the idea of an older, moustachioed version of himself. Then he put down the phone and sat unmoving, lost in thoughts about the past.

The family tree project was turning out to be much more interesting than he had expected, and he had learnt a lot. His ancestor Thomas Donnelly had been a cooper, making wooden barrels in the Guinness brewery, and another ancestor had been a hot-metal compositor in a printing works. Garrett was fascinated that such long-established and skilful jobs could suddenly be done away with. Then again, things were always changing, and maybe the computer coding that he loved and regarded as cutting edge, would also one day become redundant.

Thinking of Thomas Donnelly, his mind flitted back to the conversation he had had with Granny the previous week. The more he thought about it, the more he trusted his instinct that she was holding back on something. Garrett had made good headway tracing his roots on his father's side of the family, but on his mother's side progress had been slower.

Well maybe he could do something about that. Granny would be coming today for her usual Wednesday visit. Perhaps under the guise of asking about the craft of coopering he could prise more information from her. He rose, took the picture and made for the kitchen, eager to show Mam the photo, to await Granny, and to make another attempt at unravelling the past.

CHAPTER NINE

'Da, I'm a bit confused,' said Molly.

It was Sunday morning and Molly knew that in the period after attending Mass and before having their Sunday roast, her father tended to be at his most relaxed. Ma and Mollie's little sister, Helen, were in the kitchen, from where the mouth-watering smell of baking was wafting, and Molly had been reading her book while waiting until Da lowered his newspaper.

'What has you confused?' he asked.

'Well, are the government for Ireland, or for England?'

'How do you mean?'

Molly indicated the Sunday paper that her father had been reading. 'I saw something on the front page,' explained Molly. 'Up in Dublin they're re-opening the main bridge over the Liffey. It used to be called Carlisle Bridge, after the Earl of Carlisle, but now it's renamed O'Connell Bridge, after Daniel O'Connell.'

'That's right.'

'I know from school that the Carlisle was English, and was the Lord Lieutenant. But Daniel O'Connell was Irish, and he wanted us to have our own parliament. So why would the government change the name?'

'Good question, Molly,' said her father. 'I can see how it sounds a bit strange.'

'So why did they do it?

'They didn't, is the short answer. The government in Westminster rules Ireland. But Dublin Corporation is in charge of street names in the city.'

'So did they do it to annoy the government in England?'

Like many RIC officers, Molly's father had a moustache, and he stroked it thoughtfully now before answering. 'There might have been a bit of that,' he conceded. 'But mainly I'd say it was to honour a great Irishman.'

'You...you think O'Connell was great?'

'Most Irish people do, love,' answered her father. 'Certainly most Catholics. O'Connell got rid of the Penal Laws that made it illegal for Catholics to practise their religion, he was supposed to be a brilliant speaker, and most important of all, he was against violence. He believed parliament was where change should take place.'

'But he wanted Ireland to have its own parliament, to be independent of England, didn't he?'

'Yes, he did.'

'And...and you'd be for that, Da?'

'I would if we got Home Rule peacefully,' answered her father. 'Lots of RIC men would.'

Molly said nothing. Last night she had seen her father oiling his rifle, and there was no avoiding the fact that the Royal Irish Constabulary was an armed force. Yet Da was claiming that many RIC men favoured Home Rule for Ireland, while on the other hand the RIC were the local eyes and ears of the authorities, and their role was to enforce British rule in Ireland.

'It's possible to make progress peacefully,' said her father. 'And all aristocrats aren't the enemy of Ireland. To go back to Dublin for a moment, look what Lord Ardilaun did.'

'What was that?' asked Molly.

'He paid for St Stephen's Green park to be laid out, and then made it a gift to the people of Dublin.'

'Really?

'Yes.' Suddenly Molly's father smiled. 'Though mind you, Lord Ardilaun is also known as Sir Arthur Guinness, so the people of Dublin had given him plenty of business!'

Molly smiled back, then her father became serious again.

'It's complicated, Molly. Mr Parnell's Irish Party had a lot of support in pushing for Home Rule. But now they've joined forces with the Land League. So you've a political party, and a group that uses violence. It's not a good mix, and no one knows where it will end.'

Molly thought that if the mood in her school was anything to go by, it might end with the Land League gaining more support, and out-manoeuvring the RIC to cause havoc. Saying that would have sounded disloyal, however, so she remained silent.

'Anyway,' said her father more brightly, 'that's enough aul chat about politics for a Sunday morning. Amn't I right?'

'Yes, Da,'

'Then pop in to Mam and Helen like a good girl, and see when the dinner will be ready.'

Her father winked, and Molly smiled again. But the conversation had been unsettling, and she couldn't help but wonder what the future held.

Aidan felt excited about seeing Clara Parkinson again, but he was also a little nervous. Their secret meeting for a music session was for later in the afternoon, and now Aidan sat unobtrusively in a corner of the family's modest, white-washed kitchen, quietly practising on his tin whistle. He suspected that Clara would be a good musician, and Molly's melodeon-playing was excellent, so Aidan didn't want his own playing to let him down.

Besides the musical challenge, he was anxious that Molly and Clara would get on well. They were both friendly and bright, and possessed a sense of fun, but Aidan knew that didn't guarantee that they would hit it off. *Well we'll find out soon enough*, he thought, then he concentrated his attention on a couple of the trickier tunes that he would be playing later.

Uncle Sean had joined the family for Sunday dinner, and he and Da were sitting at the table reading portions of the Sunday paper while Ma put away the good crockery that she took out every Sunday. Aidan's sister Brigid was chatting with Ma about a dance she was planning to attend that night, and the atmosphere was warm and relaxed.

Suddenly Sean lowered the newspaper. 'Well, well, well.'

'What is it?' asked Da.

'It's Captain Boycott. He's written a letter to *The Times* in London. It's reproduced here.'

Aidan stopped practising, his curiosity aroused.

'What does Boycott say?' queried Da.

'That his blacksmith has been threatened with murder if he shoes his horses, that nobody will deliver his post, that his gates have been thrown open, his walls pulled down, and his stock driven out on the road.'

'Really?' said Da.

'Good enough for him!' said Sean. 'The man's a blackguard.'

Aidan could see that his father was troubled by the news, however. 'Even so. That letter is going to cause problems,' he said.

Aidan watched as his mother and sister stopped what they were doing, alerted by Da's sombre tone.

'What do you think will happen, Larry?' asked Ma.

'There'll be a reaction. To back Boycott. The kind of people who read that paper have power, and they won't like to see one of their own being victimised.'

'*Victimised?*' said Sean. 'The ones being victimised are the men, women, and children evicted onto the side of the road!'

'We know that. But people reading that letter will see a man being picked on. And if they're landlords maybe they'll think; *it's him today – it could be us tomorrow.*'

Aidan wondered if Clara's father would think that way, but

before he could consider it any further Ma spoke again.

'So what will they do?'

'I'd be surprised if Boycott isn't offered help to take in his crop,' said Da.

'And I'd be amazed if anyone's stupid enough to do that,' said Sean. He reached into the inside pocket of his Sunday jacket and took out a pamphlet. 'Hundreds of these are being printed,' he explained.

Aidan watched as Ma took the pamphlet.

'It's part of Parnell's speech to the Land League in Ennis,' said Sean. 'Read it out, Vera.'

Ma tilted the page to get more light, then slowly read out the message. '*When a man takes a farm from which another has been evicted, you must shun him on the roadside when you meet him – you must shun him in the streets of the town – you must shun him in the shop, you must shun him on the fair green and in the market place, and even in the place of worship, by putting him to moral Coventry, by isolating him from the rest of the country as if he were a leper of old – you must show him your detestation of the crime he has committed.*'

'That's the most powerful weapon we have,' said Sean. 'Who'll risk that to take in Boycott's crops?'

'Maybe men who aren't from the area?' suggested Da. 'Outsiders brought in specially.'

'That would cost a fortune,' said Sean

'You're not fighting an opponent who's poor,' countered Da. 'The Land League has made huge strides, but it would be a big

69

mistake to think we'll have it all our own way.'

'Maybe,' said Sean. 'But the more people who read this, the more we'll get our message across. And that's what terrifies them.'

Ma turned to her younger brother and spoke seriously. 'Be careful, Sean, about being seen giving out those leaflets.'

'Come on, Vera. The leaflet doesn't call on people to do anything illegal.'

'Even so. The RIC will be watching who's stirring up trouble. If things go bad, you don't want to be on top of their list.'

'All right, I'll be careful.' Sean suddenly turned to Aidan. 'Talking of which, not a word of this to Molly O'Hara.'

Aidan felt a flash of annoyance. 'Molly's a friend – she's not some kind of spy!'

'I'm not saying she is. But without meaning to you could let something slip when you're talking to her. And she could let something slip to Sergeant O'Hara.'

Aidan stood up, put the tin whistle into his pocket, and looked Sean in the eye. 'Neither of those things will happen,' he said. He turned to his mother. 'Can I head off now, Ma, I've done all my jobs?'

'Yes, all right, love,' she answered. 'Enjoy your music.'

'Thanks.' Aidan nodded farewell to the rest of his family, then headed out the back door. He was still annoyed at his uncle. But if Sean was concerned about Molly, what on earth would he think about Aidan meeting Clara Parkinson? Well, what he didn't know wouldn't worry him, Aidan decided. Putting it from his mind, he stepped outside and took a deep breath of the mild October air. Then he set off down the track leading away from the farm, eager to meet Clara and Molly, and to immerse himself in music for the next few hours.

The leaves on the trees were turning golden, berries were budding on the blackberry bushes, and the countryside looked glorious in the autumn sunshine as Clara made her way towards Ballydowd. Even though she was normally truthful, there was a thrill to be had in fooling her governess and family and getting away to her secret rendezvous. Clara knew that they wouldn't approve of her socialising with Aidan and his friend Molly, but she was tired of the restrictions that came with being the daughter of the Big House.

She carried a knapsack on her back in which she had her sketching pads and charcoal. Being a moderately talented artist, no one had thought it unusual when she said she was going out for a couple of hours to do some drawing. In reality, it was a cover story that enabled her to transport her violin unseen. The instrument was stored in the knapsack along with her art materials, and as she walked along Clara noted a couple of locations that she would quickly sketch on her way home, in case she was asked later on to show her drawings.

As she drew nearer to Daly's farm she recalled the directions that Aidan had given her to find the sheltered dell that was to be their meeting place. It was well away from the Daly's modest but freshly whitewashed farmhouse that she could see in the distance. Clara followed the winding track, finding herself getting slightly nervous. Supposing Aidan's friend Molly resented her joining them? Or had it in for her because she was from Parkinson House? Just because Molly was a policeman's daughter didn't mean that she would be unsympathetic to the Land League. When Aidan and Clara had spent the afternoon together last week they had chatted about their lives. But neither of them had discussed anything to do with the Land War, and Clara hoped that it would be the same today, and that they could simply meet as three people who liked music.

Turning a bend in the track, she suddenly saw the dell below her. Aidan was waiting there, standing with a girl who had wavy, jet-black hair. Aidan waved in greeting, and Clara waved back, then picked up her pace. She swung the knapsack off her shoulders as she reached the other two.

'You found the place all right,' said Aidan.

'Yes, your directions were spot on.'

'This is my friend Molly,' said Aidan. 'Molly, this is Clara.'

'How do you do?' said Clara, offering her hand.

'Hello,' said Molly shaking the outstretched hand.

She looked pretty, her lustrous dark hair flowing out from under her bonnet, and she wore a well-cut, but slightly old-fashioned coat. Clara thought, however, that perhaps the other girl was slightly uneasy, and it occurred to her that maybe Molly too was a little nervous about this meeting.

'Your hair is beautiful,' Clara said, and as soon as she uttered the words she knew she had done the right thing. Molly smiled, and immediately her demeanour seemed more relaxed.

'Thanks,' she said.

'What about my hair?' asked Aidan playfully.

'Your hair is…well, it's…well-combed!'

Aidan and Molly laughed, and Clara felt her nervousness slipping away.

'Why don't we sit down?' suggested Aidan, and Clara saw that Molly and Aidan had spread a rug along the bow of a fallen tree. The other two already had their instruments out – a tin whistle for Aidan and a melodeon for Molly – so Clara took her violin case from the knapsack and opened it.

'Nice instrument,' said Molly.

'Thanks,' answered Clara, 'it was a present for my tenth birthday.'

'Aidan says you mostly play classical music.'

'Yes, but I can pick up a tune fairly quickly. And I'd love to play something my governess hasn't approved. So I'm happy to go with whatever you normally play.'

'We could teach her "Shoe the Donkey",' suggested Aidan.

'I don't know that, but I love the sound of it,' said Clara with a grin.

Molly smiled back. 'It's a bit different to Brahms. But it's catchy, so I'd say you'll pick it up all right.'

'Fine. And just so you don't think I'm a complete stick-in-the-mud, I *can* play a few Gilbert and Sullivan tunes – my Aunt Esther often orders the latest sheet music'

'Which tunes?' said Aidan.

'I know "Poor Wandering One" and "With Cat-like Tread".'

'"With Cat-like Tread" is good fun,' said Molly, 'but I don't know the other one,'

'Then Clara can teach us that, and we can teach her "Shoe the Donkey",' said Aidan. 'Is that a deal?'

Clara thought back to this morning when she had attended Sunday School in Mullingar with other well-heeled children. Some of them were pleasant, and some of them were dull, but something told Clara that being friends with Aidan and Molly would be more interesting.

'Yes,' she said happily. 'Yes, that's definitely a deal.'

CHAPTER TEN

Garrett sat at the kitchen table, his mind racing. Dad was working late tonight, so it was just Mam, Granny and himself for dinner. But he reckoned that the smaller the group, and the more intimate the setting, the better his chances of getting his grandmother to open up about the past. Assuming there really *was* some story in the past that his grandmother was hiding. Garrett had shown his mother the picture of his look-alike ancestor Raymond Byrne, but he hadn't shown it yet to Granny, not wanting to raise the subject of the past until the moment was right. He watched her now, accepting a plate of lasagne from Mam, and he knew he had to handle this carefully.

The lasagne made him smile to himself as he remembered Granny's deceased husband, Grandda Conn. Conn had been a colourful man of strong views, who was suspicious of all foreign foods. Garrett recalled his father joking that if a dish ended with a vowel, then Grandda Conn wouldn't eat it. So no ravioli, no pizza, no lasagne, just 'plain food and plenty of it' as he used to say himself.

Looking at Granny, Garrett thought how different she was to her deceased husband. Granny was open to new foods and new experiences generally, which had made it all the more surprising when she had closed down the conversation that Garrett had started about her grandfather, Thomas Donnelly.

'Now, Garrett, here you are,' said his mother, handing him his plate.

'Thanks, Mam.' He accepted his portion, the smell of the lasagne making his mouth water. Then he turned to his grandmother, keeping his tone casual. 'Did they still have coopers making barrels in your time, Granny?'

'Of course, love. Sure they didn't replace wooden casks with metal ones until about the sixties.'

'Right. But your dad wasn't a cooper, was he?'

'No, he was a clerk. What's brought on the interest in coopers?'

'The family history project I told you about. It says on the census form that your grandfather, Thomas Donnelly, was a cooper – I thought maybe it was a trade that was passed on from father to son.'

'No, Garrett. My dad was a clerk in the civil service.'

'Do you know what department he worked in?'

'The Department of Justice. Why do you ask?'

'Maybe they'd have records from when he applied for the job. It might give us information on his parents.'

Granny had been about to raise a forkful of lasagne, but now she hesitated. 'I don't…I don't think you should waste your time there. My father was the one applying for the job. It's his information they'd have, and I already gave you that.'

His grandmother raised the lasagne to her mouth and began eating, and Garrett sensed that he was being given a signal that the topic was closed. The simplest thing would be to leave it alone. *But if he left it now that would be it. Time to take his courage in his hands and go for broke,* he decided. Garrett steeled himself, then put down his cutlery and looked his grandmother in the eye.

'Whatever happened in the past, Granny, it's no big deal today. It's so far away now, it doesn't matter what anyone did back then. If there's some…some skeleton in the cupboard, please – just tell me.'

Garrett thought he saw a flicker of annoyance in his grandmother's eyes, then it seemed to pass and she looked thoughtful. She didn't speak, however, and to Garrett's surprise the next voice he heard was his mother's.

She reached out and touched Granny's arm, then spoke softly. '*Is* there something, Ma?' she asked, 'I'm curious too. And Garrett's right, it's all far in the past now.'

'And if there is something…something private,' added Garrett, 'we can always keep it to ourselves.'

Granny looked uncertain, and Garrett held his breath, sensing that maybe they had swayed her. Then she seemed to reach a decision and she spoke calmly. 'There's no skeleton, and there's nothing to tell you. Now would you mind passing me the water, please.'

There was a slightly awkward pause before Mam responded. 'Fair enough,' she said, reaching for the water jug and pouring out a glass for her mother. She shot Garrett a glance, and he knew that she was wordlessly telling him to leave things be.

'OK, Granny, thanks anyway,' he said. But his instincts told him that something was being covered up. He couldn't push his grandmother any further, so he would need to find another route to the past. He had no idea what might be hidden there, but whatever it was, he simply had to pursue it now.

CHAPTER ELEVEN

'I had a little puppy.

His name was Tiny Tim.

I put him in the bathtub,

To see if he could swim.

He drank up all the water.

He ate a bar of soap.

The next thing you know,

He'd a bubble in his throat,

In came the doctor,

In came the nurse,

In came the lady

With the alligator purse.'

Molly swung the skipping rope with another pupil while the rest of the girls took turns to lift their long skirts, before jumping in and skipping. The school yard was alive to the sound of excited cries as the children took their morning break. Molly found the chanting of the skipping rhyme had a soothing effect, and she let her mind wander as she swung the rope.

She thought back to the meeting last Sunday with Clara Parkinson and Aidan. It had gone better than she had expected and by the time they finally parted everyone had been relaxed. As the daughter of a seamstress, Molly had recognised that Clara's clothes were top quality – she suspected her jacket design was probably in the latest style from Dublin or London. Clara had spoken too with an accent that sounded English in tone. Despite her family background, however, her manner had been genuinely friendly, and there was no doubting her talent as a musician.

Molly had been impressed by how quickly Clara had learnt to play 'Shoe the Donkey', after which she had taught Molly and Aidan to play 'Poor Wandering One' from the Gilbert and Sullivan operetta, *The Pirates of Penzance*. The time had passed quickly, and when it was time to leave Molly had been pleased when Clara suggested they meet again. During the two hours they had spent together nobody had mentioned evictions, or Captain Boycott, or the Land League, but it was still clearly understood that their gathering had to remain secret.

Thinking about it now, Molly realised that keeping things secret was actually part of the fun, and she was looking forward to next Sunday when they were to meet again. She was also excited at the thought of visiting the Parkinson estate, which was generally out of bounds to people in Ballydowd unless they were working there. Clara, however, had said there was an unused cottage in a distant corner of the grounds where they could play music. They wouldn't be disturbed there, and if the weather was cold it would be more comfortable than the dell on Aidan's farm.

Molly's reverie was broken when she realised that something

had changed in the atmosphere around her, and now she heard the sound of horses' hooves on the road that went past the school. The girl holding the other end of the rope stopped turning it, and the skipping came to a halt as the girls looked towards the road. Gradually the rest of the playground cries died down as the children watched the group that was approaching.

Molly's heart sank when she saw that it was a mounted troop of armed RIC officers who were escorting a party of bailiff's men in horse-drawn carts. The leading cart carried a battering ram, and the sudden quiet of the school yard was testimony to the fact that everyone knew that the RIC and the bailiffs were going to an eviction.

Molly saw her father mounted on the leading horse of the RIC escort and she felt her stomach tighten. Normally she would have called out a greeting to Da. But to call out a friendly greeting when they were on their way to evict a family from their home seemed wrong. Yet not to acknowledge her father didn't seem right either. Molly bit her lip, unsure what to do.

Her father solved the problem by looking straight ahead and never glancing over at the school. Molly felt relieved that there had been no interaction between them, then felt guilty for being relieved.

Nobody said a word as the police and bailiff's men passed by, but Molly sensed the silent resentment. Even the youngest pupils in the yard, who knew nothing about politics, knew what an eviction was, and what a terrible fate it was for any family. Finally, the eviction party passed, their hooves echoing down the road as they headed out of the village.

'Fair play to your father, Molly,' said Iggy Tobin. 'Doin' the landlords' dirty work. You must be really proud of him!'

Molly didn't know what to say. Although the Tobin twins were feared, they weren't actually liked by many people. Now though, Molly sensed that Iggy's jibe reflected the mood in the schoolyard. Even Aidan, who could normally be counted upon to say something to defuse the situation, seemed to be at a loss.

Peadar Tobin nodded in agreement with his brother. 'Yes, good old Sergeant O'Hara – throwing a family onto the side of the road!'

Molly wanted to explain that Da *was* a good man, that he hated evictions, that as a policeman he had no choice but to do his job. She knew though that any 'just-doing-his-job' argument would sound feeble.

Unable to face the gloating Tobin twins she turned on her heel and walked away. Reaching the far corner of the yard, she stopped and tried to gather herself. She felt terrible for the family that was about to be put out of their home and she wished that life didn't have to be so cruel. She knew that she needed to be strong if she was to face her schoolmates, but she was hit by a sudden wave of sadness. She gripped the boundary railings hard, fighting back a sob, but despite her best efforts, her eyes welled up, and slowly, uncontrollably, the tears rolled down her cheeks.

A cold October wind blew in from the east, banishing the previous mild weather with the first harsh chill of the autumn. The morning was damp and raw, the light pallid in the absence of any sign of the sun. Aidan shivered as he walked along the rutted track at the back of their farmhouse. He was using a wheelbarrow to carry swill to the pigsty, and the sour smell of the swill, combined with the numbness in his hands and feet, brought home to him again that he wasn't cut out to be a farmer.

He hadn't still told his father about his dream of working in a department store in a city like Dublin or London. On a rare trip to Dublin with his mother he had seen the imposing five-storey building that housed McSwiney's department store on Sackville Street. One look at its big display windows full of fine clothes had convinced Aidan that this was the environment in which he wanted to work. He had heard Molly's seamstress mother saying that staff in stores like McSwiney's didn't have to pay rent, but instead had free accommodation above the store. The idea of living and working with others who loved clothes and fashions had really caught Aidan's imagination, and it seemed to him like the perfect job. At the same time he understood how men like Da and Uncle Sean loved the land, and would put up with whatever hardships came with being a farmer. He feared, though, that the reverse wouldn't be the case, and he couldn't imagine them understanding his love of fine suits or his interest in trends in men's fashions.

Aidan reached the sty, his breath hanging in the air, and he began feeding the swill to the pigs. Normally he would have been in school on a Friday morning, but today wasn't a normal day. Uncle Sean had been injured yesterday in a fracas that had broken out when the RIC and the bailiffs had moved to evict the Horan family from their farm. Despite resistance from Land League activists the eviction had gone ahead, and Sean had had several ribs damaged in the clash, as well as getting cuts and bruises to his face.

Early this morning Ma and Da had set out for Sean's cottage. Ma wanted to look after her brother, and Da was planning to do whatever farm work Sean couldn't do because of his injured ribs. In the circumstances Aidan couldn't object when Da asked him to skip school today and help out on their own farm.

He would have liked to be in class to support Molly, even though he was disgusted at the role of Sergeant O'Hara in the eviction. He had always got on well with Molly's father up to now, but the idea of a big, strong man like the sergeant being involved in the eviction of women and children was disturbing. Nevertheless, Aidan had walked home from school with Molly yesterday when some of the other pupils were shunning her. It wasn't her fault that her father was an RIC man, he thought, and it was important to stand by a friend who was out on a limb.

Notwithstanding that, yesterday's events had hardened Aidan's attitude. Ruthless landlords had to be resisted, and he was proud of Uncle Sean for having the courage to stand up for what he believed in. And proud of his parents too, for immediately rallying to support him when he got injured.

Aidan tipped the last of the swill from the wheelbarrow into the trough, then stood there a moment as the pigs oinked and jostled each other while excitedly eating the swill. He couldn't get yesterday's eviction out of his head. Uncle Sean had been lucky not to be arrested in the mêlée in which his ribs had been damaged. But how could Colonel Crawford, the landlord involved, live in the warmth and comfort of his mansion, knowing that he had made another family homeless? And then another disturbing thought struck Aidan. What if yesterday's evicting landlord hadn't been Colonel Crawford? Supposing the landlord had been William Parkinson, Clara's father?

Most people in Ballydowd regarded the Parkinsons as good landlords. But with the Land War heating up, that could change, and even moderate landlords might be forced to choose sides. If that happened could he continue his blossoming friendship with Clara Parkinson? He had really grown to like her, and nobody had made any reference to the Land League when he and Molly had played music with Clara last Sunday. But how long could all three of them ignore what was going on?

As it was, there would be outrage if people knew about their secret friendship. But he couldn't let other people decide what he did, or who his friends were. And the Land War was out of his hands, so what was the point of fretting about it? Instead he would take things a day at a time, and whatever happened, happened. Satisfied with his decision, he grasped the handles of the wheelbarrow, turned his back on the slurping pigs, and started back towards the farmhouse.

CHAPTER TWELVE

Clara had never really liked Sundays. Although she didn't have lessons with her governess during the weekend she had to go to church and Sunday School each Sunday morning. She liked meeting other children at Sunday School, but the vicar's sermons could be long-winded, and Clara often had to hide her boredom.

Now, however, Sunday was turning into her favourite day. This was the third week in a row that she had secretly met Aidan, and her second time to be with Molly. Despite being nervous last week at meeting Aidan's long-time friend, the music session had gone well, and by the end of the afternoon the two girls had been chatting easily.

Besides being a talented musician, Molly had an enquiring mind, and liked reading. Clara suspected, however, that books might be an expensive luxury for the O'Hara family, and Molly had seemed pleased when Clara promised that she would lend her her own favourite novel, *Little Women*. Now the three friends were carrying their instruments as they walked along a track on a distant part of the Parkinson Estate, heading towards the unused cottage that Clara had offered as a venue for this week's music session.

The cold weather of earlier in the week was gone, and the combination of mild air, bright October light, and golden leaves on the trees made walking through the parkland a pleasure.

'Is all of this your land, Clara?' asked Molly, indicating the rolling fields stretching away into the distance.

'Eh, yes, everything as far as that tree line.'

'Gosh, it's huge. Do you know your way around it all?'

'Pretty much. When I ride out, I love to explore all the backwaters and hidden spots.'

'Right,' said Molly. 'And have you got your own horse?'

'I've a pony, Shamrock.'

'When you're not borrowing your father's horse!' said Aidan.

'Don't remind me,' said Clara with a wry grin. 'I was lucky to get away with that.'

'Here, talking about horses,' said Aidan. 'What did the teacher say to the horse when he walked into the class?'

'You know this is going to be daft,' said Molly.

'What did the teacher say to the horse?' asked Clara.

'Why the long face?'

Clara laughed despite the fact that it *was* a daft joke.

Molly laughed also, then turned to the other two as they walked along. 'So, what pieces are we going to play today?'

'I thought we might teach Clara "The March of the King of Laois",' suggested Aidan.

'Fine.'

Clara had never heard of this piece before and her curiosity was piqued. 'What's it like?' she asked.

'It's good,' said Molly. 'Although it's a march, it has a kind of flow to it.'

'Sounds great,' said Clara. 'I'll give it a try.'

'You'll do more than that, if last week's anything to go by,' said Aidan. 'Sure by the end you were playing "Shoe the Donkey" like you'd played it all your life!'

Despite knowing that Aidan was exaggerating, Clara couldn't help but feel pleased. 'Thanks,' she said. 'And in return I can teach you a Percy French song I learnt. It's called "Abdul Abulbul Amir"'

'I like the name anyway,' said Molly.

'It's great fun. And the melody's not too tricky.'

'Who taught it to you?'

'My Aunt Esther. She bought the sheet music, and we went through it together.'

Aidan looked impressed. 'You can read sheet music?'

'Yes.'

'I've been playing all my life and I wouldn't know a note on the page.'

'Me neither,' confessed Molly.

'It's hard at first. Then you get the hang of it and just read the notes,' said Clara. 'Oh, and on the subject of reading. I brought you that book I told you about, Molly.'

'*Little Women*?'

'Yes. It's in my violin case. Don't let me go without giving it to you.'

'Thanks, Clara. That's...that's great.'

'My pleasure. I'm eager to hear what you think of it – and

which of the four sisters you like best.'

'Which do *you* like best?' asked Molly.

'Definitely Jo. But don't let me sway you. Just tell me what you think when you've finished it.'

'I will – and I promise I'll keep it really safe for you.'

'Grand.'

'And now, here we are,' said Clara as they rounded a bend and suddenly came to a cottage with a thatched roof. The front door was locked, and no smoke rose from the chimney, but the building wasn't dilapidated. Clara produced a key. 'My secret den,' she said, as she opened the door. The others followed her in, then closed the door after them. There were several wooden chairs, and Clara put down her violin case on one of them and turned back to the others. 'Sorry the air's a bit musty, but the place is dry enough,' she said.

'Whole families live in worse places,' said Aidan.

Clara wasn't sure how to respond. She sensed that the comment had just slipped out, and that Aidan wasn't trying to get at her. *But what he said was true.* And evicted families didn't even have this level of modest shelter, but instead were left at the side of the road.

Clara sensed that unless she addressed the issue it would always hang over them. She breathed out then turned to face Aidan and Molly. 'I know I'm the daughter of a landlord. And I know a lot of what happens isn't fair. And even though there's nothing I can do about it, I'm really sorry. But can we all still be friends? What your father does, Molly, with the RIC, or your father does for the

Land League, Aidan, or my father does as a landowner – can we step back from that? I know we haven't been friends for long, but I really like our time together. And I'd love to get to know you both better. So what do you say? Could we leave all that other stuff behind when we get together and just...just be friends?'

Clara paused and swallowed hard. She hadn't planned to make a speech, but now that she had, she found herself badly wanting them to agree to her proposal. But was it fooling herself to think that she could shut out the nastiness of the outside world? She looked at Aidan and Molly, trying to read their expressions. A look passed between the two original friends, but Clara wasn't sure how to interpret it. It seemed to her that Aidan had slightly raised an eyebrow as though asking a question of Molly. Clara, though, had missed whatever response Molly gave, and now there was a brief silence before Aidan spoke.

'As far as I'm concerned, every word you spoke is true,' he said. 'Things *are* unfair. *Really unfair.*'

Clara's heart sank, and she said nothing in response.

'But none of us can do anything about any of that,' continued Aidan. 'So I agree with you. Let's stay friends. And when we're together we leave all the other stuff behind.'

Clara felt a huge sense of relief. 'Thank you, Aidan,' she said. 'Thank you so much.' She turned to Molly and looked at her enquiringly.

Molly raised her hands as though surrendering. 'I've put up with Aidan for as long as I can remember, and we're still friends.

I'm hardly going to stop now. And if you're a friend of Aidan's, then you're a friend of mine. So count me in.'

Clara smiled. 'That's settled then.' She offered her hand, first to Molly and then to Aidan. She knew that shaking hands might seem a bit formal, but she sensed that this was an important moment, and she wanted to mark the occasion. They all shook hands, and Clara knew, instinctively, that their futures were going to be bound together.

PART TWO

ESCALATION

CHAPTER THIRTEEN

Molly woke with a start. She sat bolt upright in her darkened bedroom, her heart pounding. She didn't know what had woken her, but she sensed that she hadn't been asleep for long. Before drifting off, she had hovered on the edge of sleep, her mind going over the day's events. She had thoroughly enjoyed the secret gathering in the cottage on the Parkinson Estate. The fun of the music-making, and the agreement that they would be friends – in spite of the trouble that was brewing – had left her feeling pleased. Now, though, her relaxed sleepiness was banished, and she strained her ears to hear what it was that woke her.

Molly was in the bedroom she used to share with her little sister, Helen, one of three bedrooms the O'Hara family had as occupants of the family quarters of Ballydowd RIC station. With her older brothers Frank and Mick working away from home, Helen had recently moved into their vacant room, while Ma and Da occupied the largest bedroom at the top of the stairs that led down to the kitchen and sitting room.

Now Molly was startled again by the sound of smashing glass. She pulled back the covers and quickly jumped out of bed. Running to the door, she opened it and stepped out onto the landing. The door to her parents' bedroom was open and the room was in darkness, so Ma and Da must be downstairs. Molly quickly descended the stairs. As she neared the bottom she saw her father pulling open the handle of the heavy door that led to the interior of the police station.

Immediately there was a whoosh of flames, and the sharp smell of smoke, and Molly realised with horror that the RIC station had been fire-bombed. She could feel the heat from the flames, then her mother almost collided with her.

'Molly!' Ma cried. 'Stand back, love!'

Stunned by the enormity of what was happening, Molly did as she was told. Her mother called after Da. 'Come back, Jim, come back!'

Instead Molly could see him flailing at the spreading fire and trying to extinguish the flames. 'Get wet blankets!' he cried over his shoulder, 'get wet blankets!'

'Quickly, Molly!' said her mother. 'Run up and take blankets. I'll get water.'

Molly saw her mother heading for the kitchen sink as she turned on her heel and ascended the stairs two steps at a time. She was terrified that Da would disregard his own safety and get badly burnt, but she knew if she gave way to fear she would be of no use to him. Instead she ran into her bedroom and reefed two blankets off the bed. She realised that her sister hadn't been woken by the commotion and she wondered if she should rouse her before delivering the blankets. *No,* she thought, *Da needed wet blankets urgently, and Helen was safe for the moment.* Molly raced to the top of the stairs then descended at speed, the blankets clutched in her arms.

'Good girl, Molly!' said Ma who was hoisting a bucket filled with water onto the kitchen table.

Molly had glimpsed her father vigorously beating at the flames inside the station. Despite his efforts it didn't look as if the fire was being extinguished, and she felt pure terror. The stone walls between the living quarters and the station proper were thick, so the fire might not spread so easily to their home. But the station interior had wooden furnishings and rafters, and if the blaze took hold then Da's life could be in danger.

Ma swiftly immersed the blankets into the large bucket, wrapped one around herself, and then ran towards the station with the other wet blanket for her husband. 'Fill the bucket again, Molly!' she cried.

Molly crossed to the sink and rapidly began filling the bucket. Before the bucket was halfway full Ma was back.

'Is Da OK?' asked Molly

'A bit singed, but he's fine. I'll finish getting the water – you go upstairs and get Helen.'

'Would it not be better if I help you here?'

'Don't argue with me, Molly! I can't help Da and worry about you two. Take her outside and wait till I come for you. Now go!'

Molly reluctantly obeyed her, sprinting back upstairs. She burst into Helen's room and scooped up her little sister, wrapping her in the bedclothes.

'Molly!' she cried waking in fear and clearly disoriented. 'Molly!'

'It's all right, but we have to get out!'

'What…'

'There's a fire,' said Molly, 'we have to get outside.' Without further explanation, Molly ran to the landing, her sister bundled up in her arms.

Helen started to cry, but Molly concentrated on descending at speed. On reaching the bottom of the stairs, Helen saw the flames and her crying intensified.

'It'll be all right' said Molly, 'it'll be all right.'

But even as she made for the kitchen door that led outside Molly knew that might not be true. Ma was no longer in the kitchen, but had gone to fight the fire with Da. Every fibre of Molly's being wanted to go to help them, but she knew that she had to follow Ma's orders and keep her little sister safe. She swung the back door open and stepped out into the cold night air.

'Where…where're Ma and Da?' asked Helen through her tears.

'They're fighting the fire.'

'They're in the fire?' Helen said, her terror obvious.

'They're putting it out,' answered Molly. 'They'll come to get us once the fire is out.'

But would they? she thought, with a sinking feeling in her stomach. Even from here she could hear the vicious crackling of the fire, and she had visions of the roof collapsing on top of them if they didn't get out soon. The thought of losing her parents filled her with despair, and she held Helen close, blessed herself, and prayed fervently that Ma and Da wouldn't die in the fire.

CHAPTER FOURTEEN

'I've good news. We found your ancestor's records.'

Garrett felt his pulses starting to race – finally, he thought, a break in trying to get more information on his great-great-grandfather, Thomas Donnelly. Garrett was on a half day from school, and was seated in the archives office of the Guinness Brewery, and the archivist had been helpful when he had explained about his school project. Now the woman looked pleased as she opened a folder. 'The timing was good regarding Thomas,' she explained. 'Back then the company was setting up a pension scheme, so they needed details on the people in the workforce.'

'And you have his details?' asked Garrett, trying to hold down the excitement in his voice.

'Yes.' The archivist slipped on her glasses then read from the file. 'Thomas Donnelly, cooper, commenced employment 28th March 1894, aged twenty-three years, retired on full pension, 27th March 1936.'

Garrett did some quick mental arithmetic. 'So he must have been born in 1871 then?'

'April the eighteenth, 1871, to be precise,' answered the archivist, referring to the folder.

'Does it say where he was born?'

'Yes, he was born in a place called Ballydowd.'

'Ballydowd? Where's that?'

'It's in County Westmeath.'

'Brilliant!' said Garrett, aware that this was a real breakthrough.

'Yes, you should be able to follow up on that,' said the archivist.

'What would be the best way?'

'Well, if you can find a birth certificate, that would tell you who his parents were. Failing that, the local church is your best bet. They'd have records of baptisms and marriages.'

'Great,' answered Garrett. The mystery of Granny's reluctance to discuss the family's past – assuming there *was* a mystery – now seemed one step closer to being solved, and he could hardly wait to follow up today's leads. 'Thank you so much,' he said, 'I'm really grateful for your help.'

'You're welcome,' said the archivist. 'I hope you find out all you want.'

'Me too,' said Garrett with a smile, 'me too!'

CHAPTER FIFTEEN

Aidan gripped the side of his school desk, struggling to keep his anger in check. Mr Quigley, the master, had left the class unattended for a few minutes, and the Tobin twins had taken the opportunity to laughingly gloat over the fire-bombing of the RIC station.

'How can you laugh about that?' said Aidan, 'Molly could have been killed!'

'She wasn't though, was she?' said Iggy, leaning back easily in his desk.

'It was the station part they set fire to, not the house,' added Peadar.

'Well, that was really decent of them,' said Aidan sarcastically. 'But supposing the fire had spread to the house – and the whole family was killed?'

'That's what they'd have got for living in an RIC station,' said Iggy.

Aidan could hardly believe his ears. He had no love for the RIC, especially since the injuries that Uncle Sean had received at their hands, but Molly was missing class today after what the family had suffered last night, and her father had been taken to Mullingar Hospital to be treated for smoke inhalation. Whatever about police lives, how could the Tobins think that risking the lives of innocent women and children was acceptable?

'*That's what they'd have got for living in an RIC station?*' Aidan repeated, looking Iggy in the eye.

'That's what I said.'

'For God's sake! Molly's twelve and her sister's five. They don't choose where they live!'

'But their aul fella does,' said Peadar. 'So, they're at risk because of him.'

'That's a really stupid argument! How can a five-year-old be a fair target because of what her father works at?'

'Who are you calling stupid?' asked Peadar threateningly.

Normally Aidan would have avoided conflict with the Tobins, but today he was too angry to be careful. 'Your *argument* is stupid.'

'So you're saying *we're* stupid?' said Iggy.

'Yes!' retorted Aidan. 'Anyone who thinks killing children is OK isn't just stupid – they're evil too!'

'No one calls us stupid!' said Peadar, angrily rising from his desk and making for Aidan. Iggy, who shared the desk with his brother, also rose, but came at Aidan from a different direction.

Aidan realised with a sinking feeling that no amount of argument would save the situation. He was going to have to defend himself as best he could against the two bigger, tougher boys.

Before he could do anything, Peadar reached him and grabbed him by the lapels. He pulled Aidan up out of the desk, but when Aidan tried to raise his fists to defend himself he found that his arms were pinioned. Iggy had come from behind and wrapped his own arms tightly around Aidan's.

Peadar roughly pulled Aidan forward until their faces were almost touching. 'Not so smart now, are you, Daly?' he said.

'Now who's the stupid one?' said Iggy into his ear.

Aidan tried to struggle free, but Iggy's grip on his arms was too strong.

'I said who's the stupid one now?' he said loudly.

Aidan realised that they wanted to humiliate him in front of the class, and he decided not to give them the satisfaction of an answer. His heart was pounding, and he could feel his knees trembling, but he would take a beating if need be rather than give in to the bullying of the Tobins.

Peadar tightened his grip on Aidan's lapels and shook him. 'Say it! Who's the stupid one now, Daly?'

Aidan could feel the other boy's stale breath in his nostrils and something inside him snapped. 'You're the stupid one!' he cried. The moment the words came out he realised that things would go badly. Even so he was taken aback by the speed with which Peadar reacted. Bunching his fist, he punched Aidan in the stomach.

Aidan doubled up. He felt a searing pain and gasped desperately for air. He could barely think straight, but he realised that Iggy was pulling him up to receive another blow. He tried to brace himself, determined to take whatever punishment the Tobins inflicted rather than beg for mercy. He saw Peadar drawing his fist back again, but Iggy still had him in a tight grip, and he couldn't squirm out of the way. Instinctively, he closed his eyes against the impending blow and tried to steel himself. The second blow doubled him up again, but even as he writhed in pain he heard a loud voice call out from across the room.

'Stop that at once!'

Aidan felt Iggy suddenly releasing him and he realised that Mr Quigley had come back into the classroom. Normally the teacher was mild-mannered, and given more to threats than physical punishment. Even with his eyes watering with pain however Aidan could see that Mr Quigley was furious. He swiftly strode towards the Tobins and without breaking stride smacked Iggy hard on the back of the neck, then pivoted and delivered a similar blow to Peadar.

'You cowardly bullies!' he cried. 'Two bigger lads ganging up on one smaller boy! Explain yourselves.'

Aidan was slowly recovering from the second blow, and as he sat back in his desk he saw that the Tobins looked deeply uncomfortable. The fact that Mr Quigley rarely got this angry made it all the more serious when he did, and the twins looked unsure how to respond.

'I won't ask you again,' said Mr Quigley.

'It was just…just a fight, sir,' said Iggy.

'I'm aware it was a fight – and a deeply unfair one. My question is what caused it?'

Neither of the twins answered, and Aidan hoped that the master wouldn't turn to him. Even though the Tobins were mean-spirited bullies, he didn't want to have to report on their behaviour in front of the whole class.

To his relief Mr Quigley kept his attention on the Tobins. Meaningfully, the master reached into his pocket and took out the heavy leather strap that he used on the rare occasions when he slapped his pupils. The teacher brought the strap down with a resounding bang onto the desk nearest to the Tobins, then spoke again, his voice soft but threatening.

'I'll ask you one more time what happened here. And if I don't get a satisfactory answer, you'll each get six of the best.'

'All right, sir,' said Peadar quickly.

Aidan had recovered enough now to pick up on the fear in his voice, and despite his own pain he couldn't help but take satisfaction at seeing a bully on the receiving end for once.

'It was an argument about what happened last night, sir. At the RIC station.'

'What sort of an argument?'

'About…about Molly O'Hara.'

'What about her?'

'Well, we…Iggy and I…we thought…we thought the RIC had it coming…with the evictions and all. And Aidan said we were stupid. So a fight started.'

'You thought the RIC had it coming?'

'Yes, sir.'

'Your classmate, Molly O'Hara, was asleep in her bed. If she'd been burnt to death would you say she had it coming?'

There was a long pause, and for the first time Aidan sensed that the Tobins might be having second thoughts.

'Well?' asked Mr Quigley.

'No, I…no, sir,' answered Peadar.

'And you, Iggy?'

Again there was a pause. Then Iggy shook his head. 'No, sir,' he said quietly.

'Finally, you see sense. Pity it's taken you so long. Because what happened last night was a disgrace. There's no one more sympathetic than me to the Land League's fight for justice. But to put the lives of an innocent family at risk is absolutely immoral. It's also terrible tactics – downright stupid in fact. So Aidan was right in his use of the word. Which is why you'll apologise and shake hands with him now. And if I ever see the two of you ganging up on another pupil, by the Lord Harry, you'll pay dearly. Now make your peace.'

Iggy sheepishly approached Aidan and limply shook his hand. 'Sorry,' he said.

Aidan said nothing, but shook his hand.

Then Peadar approached and held out his hand. Aidan looked him in the eye, but Peadar dropped his gaze. 'Sorry,' he said, then he shook hands and walked back to his desk.

'Right, back to work,' said Mr Quigley. 'English poetry, take out your books.'

Aidan reached into his schoolbag, his thoughts in a whirl. His stomach still ached, but he felt pleased that an important point had been made. As for the Tobins, they might have apologised, but he sensed that outside of school they would be even more implacable enemies in future. Well, time enough to face that when he had to. Satisfied with how things had turned out, he took out his poetry book, then sat back contentedly in his desk.

The train whistle sounded as the locomotive rattled eastwards towards Dublin, and Clara thought it was one of the best sounds in the world. To her the whistle of a train meant fast travel, and adventure, and it conjured up images from books she had read of pioneers travelling across the mighty prairies of America. Clara was sitting comfortably in a first-class compartment with her mother and Aunt Esther while the train sped through the frosty autumn landscape. Today she was wearing her new check cape with a matching hat and kid gloves, and she liked the idea of dressing smartly for a visit to the capital.

Usually she came to Dublin with her governess, Miss Andrews, when attending examinations at the Royal Irish Academy of Music. Today, however, her governess was on a day off, and Clara had come with Mama and Aunt Esther to look at wedding dress designs for Esther's marriage next spring. Esther wanted a silk dress with an elaborate train trimmed with Irish lace, and she had booked one of the leading seamstresses in Dublin to show her fabric samples today. Clara had been greatly looking forward to the trip, with the fun of a shopping expedition providing a welcome contrast to the dramatic events of the previous week.

Clara had been horrified by the firebomb attack on Ballydowd RIC station six days previously. She had heard that Sergeant O'Hara had been released from Mullingar hospital the following day, but although none of the other O'Haras had been injured, Clara reckoned it must have been a terrifying experience for Molly. Although they hadn't been friends for long, she had been taken by the other girl's friendliness and easy warmth, and she looked forward to meeting her again tomorrow. It had become too cold for fishing, but they had arranged for another secret music session in the abandoned cottage.

Fortunately Sunday night's fire hadn't spread to Molly's house, but considerable damage had been done to the inside of the police station. Almost immediately, however, repair work had been carried out. Clara had heard Papa explaining to Esther that the swift response was to send out a message that the authorities were still firmly in control. Support was also being organised for Captain Boycott, with Dublin's *Daily Express* newspaper proposing a fund, to pay for labourers to travel to Mayo to harvest Boycott's crops.

Clara wondered where it would all end. From getting to know Aidan, she had become more sympathetic to the plight of the tenant farmers and to the Land League's demands for fair treatment. But she shared her father's outrage with the extremists who had put the O'Haras' lives at risk, and who injured cattle and destroyed crops as part of their tactics.

Clara felt the rhythm of the train altering slightly and she looked out the window. She realised that while she had been lost in thought they had left the open countryside behind, and now the train had slowed somewhat as it made its way through the northern suburbs of Dublin. Clara looked at the gardens and back yards of passing houses as the train slowed further. She loved the glimpses into other people's worlds that could be had from a carriage, and she wondered what life must be like for the people who lived in these houses, as the train approached Broadstone station. In a city as big and exciting as Dublin there could be people who would go on to be world famous, Clara thought. Painters, musicians, writers – though no doubt thieves, and even murderers too, she reflected.

'Clara, you look like you're in another world!' said Esther.

'Just…daydreaming a bit.'

'Well, don't daydream your way off the train without all your stuff,' said Mama.

Clara had brought her book and a sketching pad and pencil, and she gathered them all together now as the train entered the station, plumes of smoke billowing up to the roof, and steam escaping from the engine as the locomotive finally came to a halt.

They alighted from the comfortably furnished first-class carriage and stepped out onto the platform. The tang that hung in the air was slightly harsh on the nostrils, but Clara liked its smoky flavour and the hustle and bustle of the busy railway station.

Reaching the gate, her mother presented their tickets to a railway worker. Clara could see him taking in their well-heeled

110

appearance, and she wasn't surprised when the ticket-collector nodded respectfully and said, 'Thank you, ma'am.'

Her mother nodded briskly in response, then they moved on towards the station exit. Stepping out onto the plaza in front of the station, Esther raised a hand and summoned the first driver from a line of horse-drawn cabs. The cab drew nearer, steam from the horse's nostrils rising in the autumn air.

'Where to, Miss?' asked the driver.

'Top of Grafton Street,' answered Esther.

Clara liked the atmosphere of Dublin's top fashion street, and she turned to her mother. 'Can we visit Braiden's Tea Rooms? Please?' It was Clara's favourite cake shop, and Mama smiled indulgently.

'All right. But only after Aunt Esther has conducted her business.'

'And Clara has just given me the incentive to conduct it briskly,' said Esther good-humouredly.

Just as Mama was allowing the cab driver to help her up, Clara saw the smile fade from Esther's face. A bedraggled looking woman with a baby in her arms was making for Esther.

'Please, mam,' said the woman, 'could you spare a copper?'

'Clara, into the cab!' instructed Mama.

Clara knew that her mother organised charitable works, but disliked individual charity requests like this, and avoided them as much as possible.

Clara climbed into the cab, but looked back at her aunt, who seemed unsure how to respond. 'I wouldn't ask, mam,' pleaded the woman, 'but my husband's out of work, and the baby is hungry. Please! Anything you can spare, anything at all...'

The cabman looked uncomfortable but didn't intervene, and Esther hesitated briefly, then took out her purse and slipped the woman a couple of coins.

'The blessings of God on you, mam! The blessings of God on you!'

Clara was touched by how pathetically grateful the woman was, then the cabman helped Esther into the carriage before mounting the vehicle and whipping his horse into action.

'You're kind-hearted and well-intentioned, my dear,' said Mama to Esther. 'But when you give to street beggars, it does encourage more begging.'

Esther sighed. 'Perhaps. But I'm about to spend ten guineas on a wedding dress. I couldn't refuse a desperate woman a few coppers.'

The carriage was clip-clopping down Constitution Hill towards Church Street, but for once Clara's attention wasn't caught by the lively street life of the capital. Instead she thought about what had just happened. In one way she could see her mother's point. The problems that caused people to beg wouldn't be solved by occasionally giving a couple of pennies to an individual, even though that made the giver feel better. Yet Clara's instinct was that Esther had still done the right thing.

Mama didn't argue the point any further, which Clara thought was to her credit, and for the moment they all retreated into their own thoughts as the carriage turned onto the quays, en route to Grafton Street and its upmarket shops. But the shopping expedition had lost some of its sparkle. Seeing poverty and desperation at close quarters had thrown Clara, and although she still looked forward to eating in Braiden's, some of the good had gone out of the day.

CHAPTER SIXTEEN

Molly wished the weather would be one thing or the other. Yesterday had been crisp and frosty, yet this afternoon was mild, and she felt uncomfortably hot as she walked with Aidan towards the abandoned cottage on the Parkinson estate. The unpredictable weather had matched an uncertain week for Molly. She had felt terror during the fire, relief when her father had been released from hospital, and anger at those who had started the blaze that could have killed her family. She had been further angered on hearing some of her schoolmates saying it was the RIC station that was attacked, and that no firebombs had been thrown at the family's living quarters. Strictly speaking that was true, but those who started the fire couldn't have been sure the blaze wouldn't spread, and even now, seven days later, Molly felt shaken when she thought of what might have happened.

She walked along, carrying her folded melodeon in its case, as Aidan turned to her.

'Are you OK?' he asked.

'Yes, just…a bit hot. I'm fine.' *But she wasn't really fine, however hard she tried to pretend things had settled.* She realised that she must have been quieter than usual, and Aidan had picked up on her unease. She looked at him and tried for a smile. He was a good friend, and Molly had been touched to hear of how he had stood up for her against the Tobin twins. *And yet…* Aidan's Uncle Sean was known to be a radical Land Leaguer, and as the week had gone on Molly thought that he could be involved with the people who had fire-bombed her family. That wouldn't be Aidan's fault, yet the idea that the Dalys were on the same side as those who threw the fire-bombs lingered in Molly's mind.

Now she turned around the final bend in the track, then came to the cottage, and Aidan knocked on the door. It was opened immediately by Clara.

'You're very welcome,' she said. 'Come on in.'

'Sorry we're a bit late,' said Aidan as they entered, 'but I had to finish a few jobs on the farm, and I couldn't let on I was due here.'

'It's fine, I was practising "The March of the King of Laois",' answered Clara.

Molly noticed that Clara was dressed in an expensive-looking blue velvet dress, and as she took off her coat and sat down, Molly was aware that her own dress probably cost a fraction of the cost of Clara's. She saw the other girl looking at her with concern.

'Molly, I heard about the fire, of course, but I'd no way of getting a message to you. How is your father doing?'

'He's fully recovered, thanks.'

'And you, Molly? It must have been awful…'

Molly was touched by the obvious concern in Clara's voice and she decided to answer honestly. 'I got a really bad fright, and I'm… I'm still trying to get over it.'

'It's terrible the things people will do,' said Clara.

'It is.' answered Molly. 'And…and could we talk about that?' she said on impulse. She turned to Aidan as well as Clara, and he looked at her quizzically.

'How do you mean?' he asked.

'I know we said that when we're together we'd leave all that stuff behind us, and just be friends. And I still want to do that. But what happened my family last Sunday night – it's made me think. And I feel…maybe before we can leave all the politics out… maybe we need to clear the air first. Is that all right?'

Clara nodded sympathetically. 'Of course. Anything that needs saying, let's just say it.'

'Fine,' said Aidan.

'So, what did you want to say?' asked Clara.

Molly took a breath, trying to marshal her thoughts. She hadn't planned any of this, but something in Clara's obvious concern had touched her, and made her want to be honest with her friends. 'You said…You said, Clara, that it's terrible what people will do. But it's terrible what people *have* to do. Like my father. He's kind and he's fair, and he takes being a policeman to heart. He tries to keep the peace, and protect people from criminals – but we never hear about that anymore. And he *really hates* evictions, hates putting families out of their homes. But they *make* him do it as part of his job. So, it's not just the people who threw the firebombs who make his life bad, it's those in charge too.'

'The government?' said Clara.

'And the landlords. They're the ones who demand evictions and make men like my da carry them out. And I know your father is a good landlord, Clara, but I'm angry at the landlords and I can't hide it anymore.'

'Fair enough,' said Clara quietly.

'And I might as well say it all while I'm at it, Aidan,' said Molly. 'I know your father and your uncle back the Land League. But it's almost sure to be Land League people who attacked us last Sunday night – so I'm angry with the Land League too.'

Aidan didn't reply at once, then he nodded slowly. 'Like Clara, I think it's fair enough you're angry. But I've something I'd like to say now. And maybe…maybe you've stuff, too, Clara, that you'd like to get off your chest?'

'Actually, yes, I have.'

'Then why don't we each say our bit, and …take it from there?'

'All right,' said Molly. She had no idea where this was going, and she hoped she hadn't ruined things. But no matter what happened now she was glad she had spoken her mind. And besides, if all three of them were truly to be friends, surely they had to be honest with each other. She turned to Aidan, awaiting his response.

'I see why you're angry with the Land League, Molly,' he said. 'And what happened your family was dead wrong. But if there was no Land League, farmers would be helpless. And I'm not getting at you or your dad, Clara, but landlords have far too much power. If a landlord decides he can make more money from grazing than from having a tenant farmer on his land, he can just turf him off. Did you know that in England farmers can lease land for thirty-one years from their landlord? In Ireland it's only *one* year. My da works really hard from morning to night. But we still never know from one year to the next if we'll have a roof over our heads! Will the rent go up? And if it does, and we've a bad harvest and can't afford it, will we be thrown out of our home? Will I be sleeping in a ditch, soaking wet and with no clean clothes? It's really, really unfair, and I don't think anyone should have to live like that.'

'I didn't know it was thirty years in England compared to one year here,' admitted Clara. 'And you're right, Aidan, that's really unfair never to know where you stand. But all landlords aren't the same. I know some of them don't even live in Ireland, and they just get their rents and don't care about their tenants. But there are landlords like my father who *really* care. Who reduced rents when tenants were struggling, landlords who *don't* want to evict tenants. And there are landowners who've had cattle crippled, and their crops trampled and stolen. That can't be right. So I suppose what I'm saying is that there's good and bad on both sides – with the RIC caught in the middle.'

There was a pause as though no one was sure what to do next. Molly thought that as the one who had started this she should break the silence. 'I think…I think you've got it there, Clara,' she said. 'But I want us to still be friends, in spite of everything. And… well, if you both want that, we never need to raise any of this again.'

Molly looked at Clara and Aidan, unsure what their reaction would be. Was it too much to ask that three people from differing sides could ignore those differences? She had been friends with Aidan for so long that she reckoned he and she could get through this, despite their families' opposing allegiances. But could they both stay friends with Clara with the Land War hotting up by the day?

'I'm glad we spoke our minds,' said Aidan. 'But now I'm happy to go back to our agreement, and leave all that other stuff behind.'

'Great,' said Molly. Then she and Aidan looked to Clara.

Clara nodded. 'I'm not going to be the odd one out. Let's continue as before.'

'Sure?' asked Aidan.

'As you'd say yourself, cross my heart and hope to die in a barrel of rats!'

The humorous response lightened the atmosphere, and Molly felt a surge of affection for the other girl, as well as relief that her own action hadn't broken up their little group.

'Right, now that that's settled, what are we playing this week?' asked Aidan.

'Well, I was up in Dublin yesterday,' said Clara, 'and I got two things I thought we might enjoy.'

'What are they?' asked Molly.

'Belgian chocolates and the music for a new Percy French song. Want to try them?'

'Sounds good to me,' said Molly.

'All right,' said Aidan, 'let's gorge on chocolates – and play some Percy French!'

Ma ceremoniously carried the Halloween barmbrack across the kitchen, then lowered it onto the table with a flourish. Aidan admired the way his mother somehow managed to combine cooking tasty food with doing her full share of farm work. He guessed that she was trying to keep things as normal as possible with the brack, and he thanked her.

'Smells good!' he said.

'Why wouldn't it, with the best of stuff going into it?' answered Ma.

Aidan was having tea with his parents and Brigid, the young-est of his three sisters and the only one still living at home. Even though the cottage was small, Ma kept it spick and span, and for Sunday tea she had spread a linen cloth on the table. They had been joined today by Uncle Sean, who was having his first Sunday meal with the family since his rib injury. Aidan was glad that Sean was making a good recovery, both for Sean's own sake and so that he himself wouldn't have to do additional farm work while Da helped out on Sean's farm.

Right now Aidan was in good form. After the air had been cleared at the cottage earlier today he had enjoyed the chocolates and music with Molly and Clara. Tonight too should be fun, with a huge Halloween bonfire already set on the village green and awaiting ignition. Ma cut the brack and handed Aidan a piece which he ate with gusto.

'Well?' said Ma.

'Delicious and nutritious!' answered Aidan. It was a long-standing family catchphrase, and even sixteen-year-old Brigid, who normally turned up her nose at Aidan's jokes, smiled good-humouredly.

'No sign of the ring?' asked Ma playfully, referring to the tradition of baking small wrapped items into the brack. The ring was supposed to signify getting married within a year, the cloth meant poverty, and the coin meant wealth.

Aidan grinned. 'It's the coin or nothing for me,' he said. 'And it looks like there's nothing in my slice.'

'Can't win them all, son!' said Da.

'So what are your plans for Halloween, Aidan?' asked Uncle Sean.

Aidan wondered mischievously what the look on Sean's face would be like if he answered that he was meeting his new friend, Clara Parkinson. He wasn't, of course – Clara had said she would be bobbing for apples with her family tonight – but it was entertaining to imagine Sean's reaction. Instead Aidan said, 'I'll be down at the bonfire, that's always great fun.'

He didn't add that it was the first time he'd be there without Molly, whose father thought it better this year if she avoided the bonfire. Thanks to Mr Quigley there had been no real trouble for Molly when she had returned to school, but Aidan could understand Sergeant O'Hara's desire to keep Molly away from possible conflict.

'I'll drop up to O'Hara's first though to see Molly,' he said.

'No, I…I don't think so, son,' said his father.

'Why not?'

'I know she's your friend, Aidan–' began Da.

'But her father's an RIC thug!' interjected Sean.

'Sean!' said Ma.

'What? They smashed my ribs, Vera – they *are* thugs!'

'Sergeant O'Hara did?' queried Aidan.

'His men.'

'I'm sorry, Aidan,' said his father. 'Molly's a lovely girl and she's still welcome here any time. But her father lives in an RIC barracks, and you can't be seen going there. Not the way things are right now.'

'I can't be seen going there,' repeated Aidan. 'But someone else went there – and risked burning her family to death.' Aidan was careful not to accuse Sean of anything, but he looked at his uncle.

'The walls in that barracks are two feet thick, so the family quarters were never in danger,' answered Sean. 'And the attack was made at half-nine, when the adults were still up and about. So the O'Haras weren't going to be burnt to death.'

Aidan was tempted to say that Sean seemed to know a lot about the attack, but before he could speak, his mother gently squeezed his arm.

'Da and I don't like what happened any more than you do, Aidan,' she said. 'We *really* don't. But feelings are running high, so visiting the RIC station just now wouldn't be wise.'

122

Aidan sensed that his mother was subtly distancing herself and Da from Sean's more extreme stance, but it seemed like everyone was avoiding saying anything directly. One thing was sure though – he would watch his uncle's movements very carefully in future.

'It's hard, son,' said Da, 'when people who've known each other for ages end up on different sides. But that's what happens in a war.'

'A war?'

'That's what it's turning into. We need the Land League to take on the powers-that-be. I want you to have a better future than me – and that's worth fighting for. So until the fight is over, you have to know what side you're on. Do you understand?'

Aidan thought it was more complicated than that, but this wasn't the time to say so. 'Yes,' he said reluctantly, 'yes, I understand.'

CHAPTER SEVENTEEN

'Are the rumours, true, Mr Parkinson, about Captain Boycott and his crop?'

'That would depend, Miss Andrews, on what rumours you've heard.'

Clara had been daydreaming as she travelled back from Sunday service with her family, but now her attention had been caught. It was an overcast day in mid-November and Clara was in a horse-drawn carriage with her parents, Aunt Esther, and her governess, Miss Andrews.

Her governess rarely discussed politics, and it was a measure of how much the land question was affecting Irish life that she would ask such a question.

'I heard that they've shipped in a body of Ulstermen to lift Captain Boycott's crop,' said Miss Andrews.

'Yes, that's quite true. They're in Mayo as we speak.'

Clara could tell from her father's tone that he was pleased to see a fellow landlord being supported.

'And is it also true that the police, and even the army, are standing guard over them as they work?'

'You're well informed, Miss Andrews,' said her father in what Clara recognised as a wryly amused tone. 'And yes, it was deemed necessary to protect the workers. They got hostile protests as they travelled westwards.'

'That's hardly a surprise,' said Esther. 'Shipping in workers from Ulster was always going to inflame matters.'

Clara saw a flicker of irritation cross her mother's face. 'You're surely not suggesting, Esther, that Captain Boycott be abandoned?' she said.

'No. But realistically the locals were always going to resent outsiders undermining their protest.'

'Pity about them,' said Clara's father. 'And it could have been far worse. The original plan was for hundreds of Ulstermen to travel – and to travel *armed*.'

'That would have been disastrous,' said Esther.

'Possibly. Which is why Chief Secretary Foster banned it, and insisted on a smaller, unarmed group of workers.'

'So, how many of them are there, Papa?' asked Clara.

'About fifty.'

'Fifty?' repeated Esther. 'That's got to be fewer than the number of troops and police deployed to guard them. What a ridiculous situation.'

'Easy for you to say,' answered Papa. 'You're not a landowner with a crop to harvest.'

'No, I'm the fiancée of a medical officer. And his fellow officers didn't join the army to babysit the Boycotts of this world. And besides, this must all be costing a fortune, much more than the crop is worth.'

'Sometimes a price must be paid,' said Mama firmly. 'The principle that law and order trumps mob rule is *vitally* important.'

Esther didn't have an answer to this, and as the argument fizzled out, Clara's thoughts drifted. She would be seeing Molly and Aidan later today, and their secret Sunday afternoons together had begun to be the highlight of her week. There had been no further talk about politics since the day when they had cleared the air, and the music sessions, interspersed with Aidan's silly jokes, were hugely enjoyable.

Suddenly the carriage was hit by a splatter of rain, and Clara heard a distant peal of thunder. It seemed like a symbol of more trouble on the horizon, and she hoped it wouldn't stop her getting away to the abandoned cottage this afternoon. She hoped too that the Bessborough Commission would hurry up and make the decisions that might end the Land War. She closed her eyes and said a quick prayer that the members of the commission would be fair, and that everything would work out peacefully. Aware that she could do no more, she sat back in the carriage as they entered the Parkinson Estate, and tried to relax as the horse trotted up the driveway towards home.

'What kind of things?'

Molly hesitated. Despite enjoying the secret nature of the Sunday meetings, she generally didn't like misleading her mother. *Best to keep her answer as close to the truth as possible,* 'Things like Captain Boycott,' she answered. 'A couple of months ago he was an important land agent. Yesterday he was escorted out of Mayo by the army.'

'How did you hear that?'

'It was on the front page of Da's paper this morning. It said Captain Boycott was taking the train to Dublin and that he'd be going back to England, and not returning to Mayo.'

'Right,' said Mam.

'That's a big victory for the Land League, isn't it?' said Molly.

'I suppose so. But try not to worry yourself too much, love. Eventually all this will be sorted out.'

Molly badly wanted to believe that things could be put right. Certainly the fire damage to the RIC station had been swiftly repaired. But it was one thing making a point by quickly fixing the physical damage of a fire, another thing to come up with a solution that would satisfy the landlords, the government, and the Land League.

'You really think so, Mam?'

'Yes. Dad says the Bessborough Commission is working hard, and listening to all sides of the argument. He thinks it'll suggest something that's fair.'

'But when will that be?'

131

'Sometime in the New Year, Da reckons.'

'The new year? There could be more evictions between now and then, couldn't there?'

Mam nodded sadly. 'Probably. The Land League beat Boycott, but...it doesn't mean evictions will stop.'

Molly felt bad for the families that would be evicted, but she also worried for her own family. Mam worked part time as a seamstress, and Molly knew that a good deal of her work had dried up since the land trouble had started. Even this morning after Sunday Mass, Molly had been aware of a coolness from some of their neighbours. It had grown more noticeable in recent weeks, and Molly knew it was directed at her father because of the RIC's role in confronting the Land League.

'I hate evictions,' said Molly. 'They're horrible – for everyone.'

Mam looked at her sympathetically. 'I know it's hard for you, love, because of Da's job. And I know you're bound to hear remarks in school. But I've said it before and I'll say it again. If it turns into bullying, come to me. Because I'll go down there and sort it out.'

Molly was touched by her mother's protectiveness and she reached out and squeezed her arm.

'Thanks, Mam. But I'm not being bullied. It's more...it's just some people are leaving me out of things. And there's not much I can do. You can't make people be your friends.'

'No, you can't. Then again, people who'd freeze you out like that, they're probably not worth having as friends anyway.'

Molly thought that this was true, but she still wished things didn't have to be so complicated.

'I'm sure you're right, Mam,' she said as brightly as she could. 'And don't worry, I'm fine. Like you say, everything will probably work out in the end.'

Molly went back to peeling the potatoes, hoping that she had put her mother's mind at rest, and also hoping, though less confidently, that things really would work out.

'Do you know what's impossible?' said Aidan.

'What?' asked Clara.

'To lick your own elbow.' Aidan watched as Clara and Molly immediately attempted it. 'As soon as you say it, everyone tries,' he added laughingly.

They were seated before a warm turf fire in the abandoned cottage, and the atmosphere was cosy and relaxed as they took a break from playing their instruments. Aidan had worried about Clara lighting a turf fire, whose smoke would indicate that someone was in the cottage. So far they had been lucky, and nobody had discovered their secret Sunday afternoon meetings. Their parents hadn't questioned them too closely, with the Parkinsons accepting that Clara was going off sketching, while Molly and Aidan's parents were used to them spending free time together.

Even so Aidan and Molly had been extremely careful not to be spotted entering the grounds of the Parkinson estate, but Aidan had accepted the explanation that the turf smoke was unlikely to be seen due to the cottage's remote location. The music session had gone well, with Clara teaching them how to play 'Bringing in the Sheaves', after which they had taught her the traditional air 'The Trip to Sligo'.

Aidan loved the sound they made when his tin whistle blended with Clara's violin and Molly sweetly joined in with her skilful melodeon-playing. Almost as enjoyable as the music-making, however, was the fun they had together, with Clara having a surprising repertoire of riddles and jokes.

She turned to him now and grinned. 'All right, Aidan, you got us with the elbow. But I have one for you.'

'What's that?'

'Name the only food that never spoils.'

'Surely...surely everything spoils eventually?' said Molly.

Clara shook her head. 'Not this thing.'

Aidan racked his brains. 'Salt?'

'I'm afraid not. Give up?'

'I haven't a clue,' said Molly.

'All right,' agreed Aidan reluctantly, 'I give up then.'

'Honey. They found some in a pharaoh's tomb, and you could still eat it, even after thousands of years.'

'Really?' said Molly. 'That's amazing.'

'It's true, though. Miss Andrews told me.'

'I'm not sure I'd fancy eating honey that's been in a tomb for thousands of years,' said Aidan.

'Would you fancy eating toffee that was bought in Mullingar this morning?' asked Clara, suddenly producing a bag of toffees.

'I might risk that!' said Aidan with a grin.

'Molly?'

'Yes, please.'

'It's brilliant toffee, I was tempted to buy a slab,' said Clara. 'But individual sweets are better for sharing.'

'Thanks, Clara,' said Molly

'Yes, thanks,' said Aidan, as he took a sweet. 'And talking about sharing, why wouldn't the crab share his food?'

'Why?' asked Clara, as she slipped a sweet into her mouth.

'He was a little shellfish!'

The others laughed, then the sound of sucking filled the air as they enjoyed the toffees.

Aidan thought how strange it was that just a couple of months previously he had never spoken to Clara, yet now he loved their Sunday gatherings. 'Is it just me,' he said, turning to the girls, 'or do you enjoy our get-togethers more because they're secret?'

Molly looked thoughtful. 'I love them anyway. And part of me doesn't like going behind my parents' backs – but then another part of me enjoys fooling people like the Tobin twins.'

'I'm a bit like Molly,' said Clara. 'I really look forward to Sunday afternoons. And even though I don't like pretending I'm going sketching, I love the idea of being in a secret club.'

Aidan was glad that the others also liked the secrecy of their gatherings. He wondered, though, what they would think if they knew about his other secret activity. In the weeks since the fire-bombing of the RIC station he had been keeping Uncle Sean under close observation. He still liked Sean, and had admired his bravery when he got hurt trying to prevent the Horan family from being evicted. But his attitude towards the O'Haras and the burning of Ballydowd RIC station had shocked Aidan.

He had no evidence that his uncle had been involved in the fire-bombing, but if he had been, then the danger was that he might do something like that again. And although Aidan's parents were Land League supporters they were moderate, whereas Sean's extreme approach could land the whole family in trouble. That had to be prevented, and Aidan was determined to take whatever steps were needed to protect his family.

His reverie was broken by Clara offering the bag of sweets again.

'How about another toffee each,' she suggested, 'and then we have a go at "Polly Wolly Doodle"?'

This was a lively popular song that Aidan and Molly liked and had taught to Clara.

'Fine,' said Molly accepting a sweet and taking up her melodeon.

Aidan banished for now all thoughts of spying on Uncle Sean and took another sweet. He used his tongue to slip it out of the way to the back of his mouth, then raised the tin whistle. 'All right,' he said, '"Polly Wolly Doodle" it is!'

CHAPTER TWENTY

'Tell me more about Papa when he was a boy,' said Clara eagerly.

'What can I say?' answered Aunt Esther with a smile. 'He was my big brother. Most of the time he was good-natured, other times he was a terror.'

'Tell me about those times!' said Clara.

They were finishing lunch in the smartly-appointed dining room of the Rowan Hotel, having gone into Mullingar to do some early Christmas shopping, and Esther had been reminiscing about Christmas on the Parkinson estate when she and Clara's father had been young.

'Well, this was before I was born,' said Esther, 'but the story goes that when William was about eight he got a new governess that he couldn't stand. After about a week she found a dead rat under her pillow – and gave in her notice the next morning.'

'Oh my goodness!' said Clara, her hand going to her mouth in shocked delight.

'Don't tell him I told you this,' cautioned Esther.

'I won't, I promise,' answered Clara, relishing the image of her father as a rat-wielding boy. It was such an entertaining contrast to his present role as a pillar of the community. Only this morning Clara had heard him express outrage on reading in the newspaper that Captain Boycott had been forced to cut short his stay in a Dublin hotel and make a hasty departure for the safety of London. What a contrast her law-abiding father was to the boy of his childhood, thought Clara.

'What else can you remember about him?' she asked her aunt.

'Well, as you know, he loves music, so I always remember him at the piano, and you'd often hear him singing around the house.'

'I meant other things that made him a terror,' said Clara.

Esther smiled again. 'Like I said, most of the time he was well-behaved. But I remember when he was about seventeen, he got injured by a bull.'

'What happened?'

'For a dare, William tried to sit on the bull's back and ride him like a horse.'

'No!'

'It's true. But not a word of this to your papa, I don't want him to think I was telling tales out of school.'

'I won't say a thing,' promised Clara.

'Anyhow, once he became an officer in the army, he had an official outlet for his sense of adventure. And after that he met your mother, settled down, and became a respectable landowner.'

'How did he meet Mama?'

'The same way I met Colin – during the Season.'

Clara knew that the Season was the period from April to August each year when young men and women from the upper tiers of society attended balls, soirées, and sporting events, with a view to meeting a partner.

'In your mama's case she met a dashing young army officer from Westmeath,' said Esther. 'In my case I met a dashing young surgeon from Cork.'

That made sense to Clara, who had sometimes wondered how an outgoing Irishman and the slightly reserved daughter of an English bishop were drawn together, although she had never doubted that her parents' marriage was a happy one. Just then the conversation was interrupted by the uniformed waitress arriving with the bill. Normally the hotel staff were very courteous and welcoming, but Clara had picked up on a definite reserve from the waitress when she had served their lunch. She had done nothing openly rude, but there had been a lack of warmth in her demeanour, and Clara suspected this was another manifestation of the bad feeling generated by the Land War.

Esther accepted the bill, and the waitress moved off.

'Thank you for lunch, it was delicious,' said Clara.

'My pleasure. I realised that this time next year you'll be in boarding school, so I thought we'd have a final Christmas-shopping-cum-lunch.'

'Right,' said Clara.

Her aunt picked up on her tone and looked at her enquiringly. 'Not looking forward to boarding school?'

'I don't know what it will be like, so it's…it's hard to look forward to it.'

'It will be fine,' said Esther. 'I was nervous before I went, and

I'm sure your mama was too. But you'll find your feet and make lots of new friends.'

'I hope so,' said Clara. She didn't want to say that she was fearful of leaving behind the comforting familiarity of Parkinson House, where, as an only child, she was the centre of attention. In boarding school, she would be just one of many girls. Was it very shallow of her to have reservations about that change? Perhaps, but she felt uneasy all the same. And neither could she tell Esther that she would miss her recently acquired friends Aidan and Molly.

'Approach it as an adventure,' said her aunt, 'and remember that other girls starting out will be just as uncertain as you.'

'I hadn't thought of that,' admitted Clara.

'Trust me. You might have one or two lonely moments. But a girl as bright and personable as you will do really well. All right?'

'Yes. Thanks, Aunt Esther.'

'And now we'd better set off, if we're to catch our train.'

Esther discreetly left payment for the meal in the silver dish on which the bill had been left, and they collected their coats, scarves, hats, and gloves, and left the hotel restaurant.

They stepped out into the street, the early December air crisp and fresh. Clara and Esther were well muffled up in top-quality coats, in contrast to a group of badly-dressed youths who lounged about at the nearest street corner.

Clara avoided eye contact with the rough-looking youths, and she had to step around them to get by. She was shocked when one of them snarled at her. 'Stuck up cows! But our day is coming –

and yours is ending!'

Esther quickly linked her arm to Clara's. 'Don't give them the satisfaction of even looking back,' she said.

Clara was impressed by Esther's coolness even though there was a slight tremor in her aunt's voice. 'I won't,' she said, trying hard to keep her own voice firm, as they walked away down the street.

The youths didn't follow them or call out anything further, but the unexpected nastiness of the encounter meant that Clara felt her knees trembling. The defeat of Captain Boycott seemed to have emboldened people, and Clara thought that even a year ago nobody in Mullingar would have dared to abuse a member of the gentry publicly But things were changing, and changing quickly. She walked towards the train station, forcing herself to hold her head up high, but fearful of what the future might hold.

CHAPTER TWENTY-ONE

Aidan could feel his pulses starting to race as he approached Uncle Sean's farm. It was early on Saturday afternoon, and he had told his parents that he was playing football with other boys from school. It was a convincing lie, because the local boys often had impromptu games, and although Aidan wasn't a skilful player, he usually joined in.

Aidan felt bad about being dishonest, but he could hardly tell his parents that he was spying on Ma's brother, Sean. In the weeks since the fire-bombing, Aidan had been listening carefully to everything Sean said and watching his every move. There was no doubt that his uncle was on the extreme wing of the Land League movement. But Aidan hadn't come up with anything linking Sean directly to the attack that could have had fatal consequences for Molly and her family.

Today Uncle Sean was attending a protest rally in Mullingar, providing Aidan with a rare opportunity whereby his own free time coincided with his uncle being gone for a few hours. Even so, Aidan felt nervous as he reached the small, slightly ramshackle cottage where Sean lived. He went around to the rear door, which he knew was never locked. Just in case Sean's plans might have changed, Aidan knocked on the door and called out in greeting as he passed though a tiny scullery and entered the empty kitchen-cum-living-room. There was no fire lit in the grate, and the house felt cold.

The other room in the cottage was Sean's bedroom, and with the door open, Aidan could see that it too was empty. His heartbeat slowed a little, but if his nervousness had lessened, now he felt bad for invading Sean's privacy by searching his house. *Come on,* he told himself, *you've come this far, you have to go through with it.* In truth, Aidan wasn't sure what he was hoping for, though at the back of his mind was the fear that he might uncover fire bombs, or guns and ammunition.

He started at the far end of the kitchen–cum–living room, opening drawers in the dresser that ran along one wall, and being careful to replace everything exactly as he found it. The drawers held cutlery, twine, brown paper, a bottle opener, and assorted keys, some of them so old that they were rusting.

He opened presses, looked under cushions, checked if anything was hidden in the large turf bucket that stood before the fireplace, but all to no avail. Aidan moved on to the bedroom. The room was untidy with the bed unmade and Land League pamphlets piled haphazardly on a bedside table. Aidan looked under the bed, finding nothing but an empty chamber pot. He carefully lifted the mattress in case anything was hidden there, and when that yielded nothing he checked under Sean's pillow. He painstakingly went through Sean's clothes in a battered wardrobe. Unlike Aidan, Sean had no interest in clothes or fashion, and his worn garments reflected this. Aidan then moved to a small chest of drawers in which were socks, vests and underwear. He was hit by another pang of unease, but he told himself that invading Sean's privacy paled by comparison with the fire attack that could have ended his friend's life. He was relieved though when he finished going through Sean's personal items with the search yielding nothing.

Aidan moved back into the living room, then paused. He tried to think where he would hide something if he lived here. *Would he keep it in the cottage or use one of the outhouses?* Before he had time to figure it out, he was badly startled by a series of knocks on the front door. Aidan felt his heart suddenly hammering in his chest, and he stood stock still. He could feel his knees trembling, but he took a deep breath and tried to think clearly. Obviously Sean wouldn't knock on his own hall door. A neighbour might though. And if he was dropping something back and Sean wasn't at home the caller might enter through the back door. Then Aidan would be caught. The knocking was repeated, and he stood unmoving, his mind racing. If a neighbour did enter, maybe Aidan could say that he had just dropped in on his uncle? But how would he explain standing like a statue and ignoring the knocks?

Before he could consider it further, he saw movement at the window and flattened himself against the wall. He reckoned that he hadn't been seen, and he prayed that the caller would go away. He held his breath, hoping to hear retreating footsteps. Instead he heard the back door opening. *He was going to be discovered.* And just when he needed to talk his way out, he felt his mouth going dry. *No,* he thought, *I mustn't panic. Better to be brazen. Go meet the intruder and try to take the initiative.*

He stepped away from the wall, steeling himself to walk confidently towards the scullery. Just then he heard the sound of something landing on the scullery floor, followed by the bang of the back door closing.

What was going on? Forcing himself to act, he stepped away from the wall and suddenly everything became clear. On the scullery floor was a large, stamped brown envelope. Aidan breathed a huge sigh of relief, then quickly crossed to the front window of the cottage. He peeked carefully out, in time to see the retreating figure of the uniformed postman.

Aidan waited a few moments until the postman was well gone, then he exited from the rear of the cottage, stepping over the envelope and closing the back door.

He crossed the yard, and spent the next few minutes searching the tumbledown outhouses. He carefully moved and replaced empty wooden crates, and checked underneath abandoned farm implements and broken harnesses. He was walking past a broken feeding trough when his eye was caught by two sacks casually thrown in the corner. The sacks were labelled chicken feed, and Aidan stopped in his tracks. For a farmer to store chicken feed was entirely commonplace. *But Sean didn't keep chickens.*

Feeling a flutter of excitement Aidan moved to the sacks and opened the top of the first one. He was hit by the familiar smell of feed, a smell he had never liked. Nevertheless he plunged his hand down into the sack. He moved his hand around, but felt nothing untoward. The sack was quite deep, and so Aidan persisted, and forced his hand further down. Splaying his fingers, he groped around, then his hand closed on something hard. It was wrapped in rough sacking, but by pulling upwards Aidan was able to extract it from the chicken feed.

Aidan undid the sacking and to his surprise found two heavy police batons and a pair of handcuffs. *What on earth was Sean planning to use these for?*

Aidan laid the implements aside. Before he left he would replace everything, but for now he was eager to search the second sack. Opening the top, he quickly sank his hand deep into the sack. This time he came across the hidden contraband on his first try. His hand closed around another piece of rough sacking and he pulled upwards until the package came free, spilling chicken feed onto the ground in the process. That too would have to be cleared up, but first Aidan had to know what had been hidden. Swiftly undoing the sacking, he exposed the hidden contents. *No!* he thought, *no!* He swallowed hard, not wanting to believe his eyes. Any doubt he had about Sean's attitude to violence was swept away, as he looked, with horror, at twelve carefully wrapped sticks of dynamite.

CHAPTER TWENTY-TWO

Garrett loved travelling by rail, but today's journey was more enjoyable than most. He was comfortably seated on an intercity train with his mother, and they were speeding through the spring countryside towards Ballydowd. The sun-dappled midlands glided by outside the carriage window, and the waters of the Royal Canal sparkled as the train travelled westwards, parallel to the route of the waterway.

Garrett was interested in transport and he knew that the canal had been built over two hundred years ago, linking Dublin with the River Shannon. He thought how much change the route had seen – firstly with barges pulled by horses, then driven by steam engines, then the canal itself overtaken by rail transport, until that too was overtaken by the car. He was glad that for environmental reasons rail travel was once again increasing in popularity. He had done some research online and discovered that the main line to Galway on which he was travelling had been opened in 1851. Did that mean his ancestor Thomas Donnelly used this very line when he went up to Dublin? It seemed quite probable, and Garrett liked the idea that all these years later there was something that he had in common with his great-great-grandfather.

Garrett was still being good-humouredly mocked by his friends over his resemblance to his other, moustachioed relative, Raymond

Byrne. Supposing by another fluke of genetics he also looked like Thomas Donnelly? Not that it was likely that he would find out. Granny had photographs of her parents, but nothing going back another generation to Thomas and his wife. Or so she said. Garrett was still unsure about whether or not Granny was being honest in her claim to know so little about her grandparents. Well, time would tell, he thought, and today could be the day when he got some answers.

'Not long now,' said Mam, breaking his thoughts, 'we're slowing down.'

'Great.'

'Excited?'

'Yeah,' replied Garrett. 'It would be brilliant to get to the bottom of everything.'

'Don't build your hopes up too high,' said his mother gently. 'I mean, I'm dying to know too. But we're going back a long way – who knows what the records might be like.'

'I know, Mam, but…I just have a feeling the answers are in Ballydowd.'

'We'll find out soon enough,' said Mam as the train pulled into the station and drew to a halt.

Garrett and his mother got off with several other passengers, and he saw that the station was small, but neatly kept. Someone had planted colourful flowers, and the wall behind the station name was freshly white-washed and gleamed in the sunshine. Garrett wasn't superstitious, but he still thought it was a good omen that Ballydowd station looked so welcoming.

They left the platform and walked out the exit, and Garrett was surprised to find that they weren't in the village. Instead the rail halt was located in the countryside. 'Where's Ballydowd?' he asked.

'Seems like it's a kilometre away,' said Mam, pointing at a signpost.

'Why would they build the station so far from the village?'

'Good question, Garrett. Though actually quite a few stations are on the outskirts of towns and villages – don't ask me why.'

'So we have to leg it for a kilometre.'

'God love you,' said Mam playfully. 'Sure isn't it terrible to ask a fit fourteen-year-old to walk a kilometre!'

'It's not so much the walk, it's…'

'What?'

'I just want to get there. And see can we solve the mystery.'

'Fair enough. Well, only one thing for it,' said Mam. 'Let's step it out for Ballydowd.'

'OK,' said Garrett eagerly. 'Let's step it out.'

CHAPTER TWENTY-THREE

'Enjoy your day off tomorrow,' said Mr Quigley to the class. 'But have all homework done when you get back on Thursday, or there'll be skin and hair flying!'

Although it sounded like a threat, the teacher had spoken good-humouredly, and there was an air of relaxation among the pupils as school broke up for the day. Molly was looking forward to tomorrow, the eighth of December, a church holiday when people traditionally took time off to visit the nearest big town and do their Christmas shopping.

Normally Molly walked home from school with Aidan, but he hadn't shown up today. She hoped he wasn't sick, but reckoned that it was more likely that he was needed for something on the farm. She made for the classroom door and was exiting into the schoolyard when a voice called out, 'Hey, Molly! Wait for us, we'll be with you.'

It was Iggy Tobin who had called her, and he was accompanied as usual by his brother, Peadar. Molly hesitated. Although the Tobins walked the same route as her from the school to the centre of the village, she rarely travelled with them. But with Aidan absent it would seem very pointed if she refused to walk with them now. Since the talking-to that Mr Quigley had given the Tobins they had eased off from giving Aidan and Molly a hard time. She still didn't trust them, but there was no point antagonising them need-lessly, and so she waited until they fell into pace beside her, their worn boots clattering as they crossed the yard.

'So, how are you?' asked Iggy, his breath visible in the damp winter air.

Molly knew he didn't care how she was. But she didn't want the Tobins to be aware that she was on her guard, and she kept her voice neutral. 'I'm fine.'

'Are you?' said Peadar with mock sincerity. 'Well, that's good.'

Molly knew she shouldn't respond, but she couldn't help her-self. 'Why wouldn't I be fine?'

'Well, that's the thing,' said Iggy. 'A lot of people like you *wouldn't* be fine.'

'People like me?'

'The daughter of an RIC man,' answered Iggy.

'Living in an RIC station,' added Peadar.

They had left the school yard and reached the road, and Molly came to a sudden halt. 'We've had all this before. But if you've something new to say, just spit it out.'

'You mean you haven't heard the latest?' asked Iggy.

'The latest what?'

'The latest *eviction*,' said Peadar. 'Just a couple of miles out the road this time. Jamsie Nolan and his family are being put off their farm.'

Molly couldn't hide her shock.

'Daddy didn't tell you that, did he not?' said Iggy.

Molly didn't know what to say. Her father had said nothing about an eviction as local as this. But if Iggy and Peadar knew, then Da obviously knew too, but hadn't mentioned it at home.

'I'm not surprised he kept it quiet,' said Peadar. 'I'd be ashamed of me life too.'

'Yeah, one Irishman stabbing another Irishman in the back,' added Iggy.

'My father's never stabbed anyone in the back!' said Molly spiritedly. But she couldn't muster any argument in favour of a family being made homeless. And she was annoyed too at Da for not letting her know that this was going to come up. The longer she stayed with the Tobins the worse it was going to get, so she turned her back on the twins and walked away at speed.

'That's right, run away!' cried Peadar.

'Back to your nice warm house, paid for in blood!'

Molly walked away as fast as she could, ignoring the taunts. It didn't take her long to reach home and she hoped that her father would be in the barracks. As the local sergeant he had to deal with a lot of paperwork that he often wrote up at this time of the afternoon. Molly entered the station and exchanged greetings with the constable who was manning the desk. 'Is my da here?' she asked

'In his office.'

'Thank you.'

Molly crossed to the door and knocked.

'Come in,' called her father from inside the room.

Molly entered and saw Da sitting behind his desk, a welcoming coal fire burning in the grate beside him. He lowered his pen and regarded her with surprise.

'Molly. What brings you here?'

Molly closed the door so that the constable wouldn't hear, then looked her father in the eye. 'Is it true, Da, that the Nolans are going to be evicted?'

'Who told you that?' he asked, looking uncomfortable.

'I heard it in school. Is it true?'

Her father nodded reluctantly. 'Yes. I'm sorry, love, but they're persistently behind with their rent. So Mr Campbell, the landlord, has called time on them.'

'Coming up to Christmas, he'll put a family onto the side of the road?'

'I know, it's a horrible situation.'

'It's not just horrible, Da. It's wrong.'

'You don't know all the details, Molly.'

'Then tell me. Please.'

Her father hesitated, then seemed to reach a decision. 'I grant you, it's very harsh, and I don't agree with Campbell's hard line. But Jamsie Nolan isn't blameless. He can find the money to have a pint in Murray's bar, but not to pay his rent.'

'Does he...does he drink a lot?' asked Molly.

'Not that much, to be fair. But he shouldn't be drinking at all when he can't keep a roof over his family's head.'

Molly found herself torn. She knew that small farmers like Jamsie Nolan did backbreaking work in all sorts of weather. It didn't seem unreasonable to her if he occasionally enjoyed a drink. On the other hand if a choice had to be made, Molly knew her own father would put his family first, and she thought that Jamsie should have done the same. Before she could give it any more thought, Da spoke.

'Sit down, love. I don't want you worrying more than you have to, so there's something I'm going to tell you.'

Molly sat and looked expectantly at her father.

'I shouldn't really be saying this, so you've got to keep it to yourself, all right?'

'All right, Da.'

'We have sources – people who pass us on information. And we've heard that there's talk of a fund being raised.'

'Raised for what?'

'To help Jamsie Nolan pay his rent. If they raise the money, and if Mr Campbell accepts it, which is not a given-'

'The eviction wouldn't go ahead?' said Molly eagerly.

'Yes. That would solve so many problems. For the Nolans, for the RIC, for the whole community around here.'

'Do you think that's what will happen?'

'I'm hoping that's what will happen. In fact, I'm praying that it will.'

'Then I'll pray too, Da,' said Molly solemnly. 'I'll pray too.'

Clara sat before a crackling log fire in the drawing room and thought how lucky she was. Earlier she had gone for an invigorating canter around the estate on Shamrock, her pony, then soaked in a hot bath before dressing in fresh clothes and coming down for afternoon tea with her family. Cook had made delicious scones that were still warm, and Clara savoured the taste of tangy blackberry jam and melting butter as she bit into her scone.

She had always known that her position was a privileged one, but her recent insight into the lives of Aidan and Molly had brought home just how fortunate she was. With a large staff of farm workers, stable hands, and servants meeting their needs, the Parkinsons enjoyed a very comfortable existence. Even the way they shopped for Christmas illustrated for Clara how different the gentry were from the local people. Aidan and Molly would be celebrating today's Catholic feast day by doing their Christmas shopping with their families in Mullingar. The Parkinsons, by contrast, would travel to Dublin closer to Christmas and buy their clothes and gifts in the fashionable, upmarket shops of Grafton Street.

Clara was glad that they wouldn't be shopping in Mullingar. She had been upset by the incident there when the boys had shouted abuse at her and Aunt Esther. She still travelled to Mullingar every week to attend elocution and drama lessons, but she no longer felt as comfortable as she used to before the Land War changed the mood in the town.

Still, she wouldn't dwell on that now, she decided, as she took another bite from her scone. Today they were making plans for the ball that Mama and Papa hosted every December. The Parkinsons' Christmas ball was a popular event, and members of the gentry from all over Westmeath and beyond attended each year. Some of them could be a little aloof – she had never liked Colonel Crawford, the landlord involved in the eviction last October – but most of them arrived in festive mood, and dressed in their finery. It was one of Clara's favourite things about Christmas, and she loved watching the glamour and style of the ladies as the occupants of each carriage were announced on entering the ballroom.

'So, Clara, shall we draw up the list of entertainment?' said her father now, lowering his teacup and looking at her with a smile.

It was traditional that at the Christmas ball members of the Parkinson family performed party pieces during the course of the evening, and Clara's father and mother, along with Aunt Esther and the governess, Miss Andrews, had gathered over tea to discuss this year's entertainment.

'Yes, let's draw up a list of victims!' answered Clara.

'Starting with yourself perhaps?' said Esther.

'Well…'

'Might I suggest the Chopin Prelude?' said Miss Andrews. 'You play it beautifully.'

'I thought I might play the violin this year,' said Clara.

'If you'd prefer that, dear, then of course,' said her mother. 'What would be a suitable piece, Miss Andrews?'

'Perhaps…Schubert's Serenade?' suggested the governess.

Although she liked the Schubert piece, Clara thought the

choice should be hers. What would they say if she suggested 'Shoe the Donkey'? she thought mischievously. Of course she couldn't reveal that Aidan and Molly had taught her the Irish dance tune, but it was amusing to imagine their faces were she to propose 'Shoe the Donkey' instead of Schubert.

'Is that agreed then?' asked her father.

No point being silly, she thought. 'Yes, Papa. Schubert's Serenade it is.'

'Fine. Perhaps your contribution next, Esther?'

Clara's mind drifted a little, and she finished her scone, then helped herself to a shortbread biscuit as the members of her family discussed what they might perform. This would be the last of these Christmases, she thought. Next year she would be at boarding school and wouldn't arrive home until much nearer to Christmas Day. And with the reforms being demanded by the Land League, who knew how many of tonight's guests might decide they no longer wanted to be landlords?

Change was in the air, and nothing could be taken for granted. Well, so be it, thought Clara, sometimes change was needed. Meanwhile she would enjoy this Christmas for what it was and let the future take care of itself. She took one last shortbread biscuit, popped half of it into her mouth, and looked forward to the Christmas ball.

'Now, one toffee apple. Get that inside you!'

'Thank you very much,' said Aidan, accepting the apple from his uncle. They were in the main street of Mullingar, and the thoroughfare was filled with other farm families like the Dalys, all paying their Christmas visit to town. The shops were busy, their windows aglow with light in the late afternoon, and street traders were selling food, drinks, and bric-a-brac from stalls.

On impulse Uncle Sean had bought two toffee apples, one for Aidan and one for his sister Brigid, while Ma and Da smiled indulgently. All of them had come into Mullingar for late morning mass, then spent the rest of the day in town, enjoying the novelty of spending time together in a holiday atmosphere.

Buying the toffee apples was typical of Uncle Sean, who didn't have much money, but was always generous with what he did have. Ma had always claimed that her side of the family had a capacity for fun, and Sean was entertaining company, which made it all the harder for Aidan to deal with his confused feelings for his uncle. It was four days since Aidan had found the dynamite, and despite his horror at the discovery he had told nobody.

He had wrestled with his conscience, unsure of what was the right thing to do. If he went to the police Sean would be arrested and sent to jail. He couldn't bring himself to inform on a member of his own family, especially when Aidan actually admired the Land League's goals. But if he said nothing would he be partly to blame if his uncle used the explosives and someone was killed? No, Sean was a hothead, not a murderer, he told himself, and if his uncle ever used the dynamite it would be to blow up a building, not a person.

Aidan had also considered telling his parents about the dynamite. But eventually he had decided that that would only be shifting the dilemma over what to do from his shoulders to theirs. And he would be sure to get into trouble with Ma and Da for snooping in his uncle's cottage and sticking his nose in where it didn't belong. In the end he opted to do nothing for the moment, and he consoled himself that he hadn't found any of the firebombs whose use had put Molly at risk. Aidan's thoughts were interrupted now by his sister light-heartedly asking a question.

'Uncle Sean, would you say the dentist is in cahoots with the toffee-apple man – to drum up business?!'

Aidan had bitten into his own toffee apple and it *was* extremely sticky and sweet, and was already adhering to his teeth.

'That's the thanks I get,' said Sean. 'But if you like, I'll take it back and eat it for you?' he added playfully.

'That's OK,' said Brigid, 'I'll chance it!'

The others laughed, then the family continued their amble along the busy street. Brigid linked arms with Ma, and Aidan fell into step alongside his father and uncle. Everyone around them was dressed in their Sunday best, and Aidan noted admiringly the overcoats, cloaks, and hats that the shops were showing in their window displays.

It had occurred to Aidan that today might provide a natural opportunity to bring up the subject of clothes and his interest in the drapery business. 'I love this,' he said now.

'Love what?' asked Da.

'December the eighth. Everyone dressed in their best and looking smart. It makes things feel special.'

'It's a welcome break, all right,' said Sean.

'And I love the way the shops have all the good clothes in the windows. They look great.'

'They do,' agreed his father.

Aidan felt encouraged. He was about to guide the conversation further in this direction when his uncle spoke.

'Still, I'll be happy enough to change back into my normal clothes.'

'True for you,' agreed Da. 'We'll leave the fancy duds for the toffs!'

Aidan was disappointed. He tried not to let it show and bit distractedly into his toffee apple. There was no point now in raising the prospect of working in the drapery business – the timing definitely wasn't right.

'So what's the latest on Jamsie Nolan?' asked Da, the topic of clothing already forgotten.

'The situation's on a knife edge,' answered Sean. 'We think we'll just about raise the rent money, but we don't know if they'll take it or not.'

'Let's hope for the best,' said Da.

'Hope for the best, prepare for the worst,' said Sean.

Neither man said anything more. Aidan felt his earlier sense of wellbeing draining away. He was disappointed by Da's out-of-hand dismissal of fine clothing, and now Sean was talking of preparing for the worst. Aidan bit once more into his toffee apple and tried to forget his worries, but there was no getting away from it – the magic of the special day was over.

CHAPTER TWENTY-FOUR

'You should have rung in advance,' said the sacristan. 'Given me a bit of notice.'

Garrett and his mother were in the parish church in Ballydowd. The air was scented with candlewax, and the midday sunlight shining in through the stained glass windows bathed the quiet church interior in a warm glow. Garrett was impervious to the atmosphere, however, as he looked anxiously at the sacristan. If she chose not to be co-operative then the journey to Westmeath would be in vain.

Garrett studied her, trying to work out how best to respond. She was a small, stout woman in her late sixties with tight, heavily permed hair. She wasn't exactly unfriendly, but Garrett sensed that saying anything that got on the wrong side of her would be a big mistake. Before he could come up with a reply Mam spoke.

'You're absolutely right, of course, we should have rung before coming down. And I'm sorry to be bothering you, I'm sure you've lots of responsibilities. But seeing as we've travelled all the way from Dublin, we'd be hugely grateful if you could find a few minutes to look at the records.'

Mam's tone was persuasive, and Garrett had to concede that having his mother along might turn out to be a good move.

'Well, I suppose I could take a look,' said the sacristan. 'What was the name again?'

'Thomas Donnelly,' answered Garrett.

'And thank you so much for your help,' said Mam.

'That's all right,' answered the sacristan, who seemed to have softened a little. 'Do you know when Thomas was born?'

'Yes,' said Garrett, 'April 1871. We couldn't get a birth cert, but we hoped there might be a Baptismal record here that would give us his parents' names.'

'It's good you have the date,' said the sacristan. 'If he was born in April 1871 he was probably baptised shortly afterwards, so I can look at those records.'

'Great!' said Garrett.

The sacristan raised her hands in warning. 'Don't get your hopes up too high. There's no guarantee with stuff like this. It's a hundred and fifty years ago, so the records mightn't be complete, or the family could have moved after the birth, and he could have been baptised somewhere else.'

'Yes, we do understand that,' said Mam.

'Good. Having said that, there's a fair chance we'll find something. So if you want to hang on here I'll see what I can dig out.'

'Thanks,' said Garrett, his excitement starting to mount, 'thanks a million!'

CHAPTER TWENTY-FIVE

'I've a good trick for you,' said Molly.

'What is it?' asked Clara eagerly.

Molly liked the way her friend was always open to anything new at their secret Sunday gatherings in the abandoned cottage. It was a bleak day outside, but the fire warmed the one-room cottage and scented the air with a pleasant peaty smell. They were relaxing now, halfway through their music session, and had taken a break from playing.

'Remember when Aidan said you couldn't lick your elbow?' Molly asked. 'Well, I've another thing no one can do.'

'What?' he said.

'First of all, hum a piece of music.'

Clara and Aidan both hummed, then Molly raised her hand.

'All right,' she said, 'you can stop now. When I tell you, try to hum again, only this time squeeze your nose tight. Go.'

Clara and Aidan did as instructed, and Molly burst out laughing when no sound emerged from their mouths.

'What did I tell you?' she said.

Aidan looked bemused. 'Not being able to hum – it feels weird.'

Clara nodded in agreement. 'I tried hard, but it just made my ears pop.'

'I don't know how it works,' conceded Molly, 'because when

you hum the sound seems to come for your mouth.'

'Yet when you close your nose it stops dead,' said Clara.

'Well, thanks for that, Molly,' said Aidan with a grin. 'I'm sure at some stage in our lives it will come in useful.'

'Talking of useful,' said Clara, 'I learnt something good at Sunday School this morning.'

Molly was surprised. She knew Clara liked meeting other children each Sunday morning, but also that she found the vicar dull. 'I thought...I thought you didn't really like Sunday School?' she said.

'Sometimes I do and sometimes I don't,' answered Clara. 'But this morning I learnt a riddle and a joke from one of the other girls.'

Molly looked at her friend. 'Try us then.'

'All right. What lies on its back, a hundred feet in the air?'

'I've no idea,' said Aidan.

'Molly?'

Molly thought a moment more then shook her head. 'No, you've got me.'

'A dead centipede,' answered Clara triumphantly.

Aidan groaned. 'Please tell me that wasn't the joke!'

'No, silly, that was the riddle.'

Molly thought it was a decent riddle and she smiled at Clara. 'Not bad,' she said. 'So, what's the joke?'

'What do you call a girl with a frog on her head?'

'What?' asked Molly.

'Lily!'

It wasn't a great joke, but Molly was mildly amused, and she laughed for Clara's sake.

Aidan, though, put on a look of mock seriousness. 'I've definitely heard a worse joke at some time in my life,' he said, 'I'm just not sure when.'

'Aidan!' cried Molly, but now he smiled, and it was clear that he was play-acting and that Clara wasn't offended.

'I wish I was better at telling jokes,' she admitted. 'I know I'm not great at it.'

'Sure we all wish for something,' said Aidan. 'I wouldn't worry about it.'

'I won't,' said Clara. Then her expression became more serious. 'But seeing as it's come up, what do you wish for, Aidan? Joking aside.'

Molly had noticed before that although Clara was good fun, she also had a deeper, reflective side. Maybe it came from being an only child, and spending a lot of time on her own, Molly thought. Whatever the reason, Clara sometimes asked questions like this, and Molly looked with interest at Aidan as he pondered the question.

'Joking aside?' he said. 'I wish my da wasn't so set on me being a farmer.'

'You don't want to be a farmer when you grow up?' asked Clara.

'No. I'd love for us to *own* the farm – but not with me running it.'

'What would you like to be?'

Molly could see Aidan hesitating for a moment, then he obviously decided to trust Clara with his dream.

'Do you know McSwiney's?' he said.

'The big store on Sackville Street?'

Aidan nodded. 'I'd love to work in that kind of department store. In Dublin, or maybe even London,' he said. 'Selling men's clothes, buying in the latest fashions for our customers, displaying them in the windows – all that kind of stuff.'

Molly knew that she was the only other person with whom Aidan had shared his vision, and she hoped that Clara would respond positively.

'You're surprised,' said Aidan.

'A little,' answered Clara. 'But I think it's a great idea, and I'd say you'd be brilliant at it.'

Aidan looked touched by the sincerity of the compliment, and Molly was pleased that Clara had said the right thing.

'And what about you, Molly?' asked Clara, turning to her. 'What would you wish for?'

Molly realised that she should have seen the question coming and her mind raced as she tried to provide an answer. In truth, her first wish had already been granted when she had heard that the Nolan eviction had been halted for now. The money for the rent had been raised in the community, and the landlord, Mr Campbell, had accepted it. It wasn't clear what would happen in January, but this month had been sorted out, which meant that the Nolan family would be secure in their home for Christmas, and

Da wouldn't be involved in their eviction.

Molly was reluctant to bring local politics into their Sunday gathering, so she framed her answer carefully. 'My wish would be that the Bessborough Commission will come up with something that's fair. Something both sides can accept so there's peace again, and my dad won't have to be in danger.'

'I hope that comes to pass, Molly,' said Clara, 'I really do.'

'And what about yourself?' asked Aidan. 'What do you wish for?'

'Well, if Molly's wish for peace works out, then I can pick something just for myself, can't I?' said Clara.

'Absolutely,' answered Aidan.

'And...seeing as you've both been honest, I'll tell you something I haven't said to anyone before,' said Clara.

'Yes?' said Molly her curiosity whetted.

'I'd love to play one day in an orchestra. As a full-time musician. Mama and Papa wouldn't think that a suitable role for a lady, but if I had my wish, that's what I'd love.'

'You'd be great at it,' said Aidan. 'You're very talented.'

'He's right,' added Molly. 'You could hold your own with any musicians.'

'Thank you,' said Clara. 'I...I really appreciate that.'

'It's the truth,' said Aidan.

'Well, if I'm going to be a musician,' said Clara with a smile, 'I need to play a lot of music. So, what are we doing next?'

Molly looked at Aidan and Clara and felt pleased that their

friendship had deepened to the point that they could share their dreams. Now though it was time to get back to playing, and she picked up her melodeon. 'Why don't we have a bash at "My Grandfather's Clock"?' she suggested.

'OK,' said Aidan. 'Bashing it is!'

CHAPTER TWENTY-SIX

Clara felt a mixture of emotions as she stood at the entrance to the ballroom. Her home was filled tonight with the leading members of local society, and there was a festive air as the guests mingled at the annual Parkinsons' Christmas Ball. Clara thought the house looked splendid, and she was proud of her family home, and how Mama and Papa and the servants had gone all out to have it looking so well. Mixed with her pride was nervousness at the idea of performing Schubert's 'Serenade' before all of the guests, but she was also excited, both by the glamour of the ball and the chance to play in front of what she knew would be a supportive audience.

Clara was wearing a new velvet dress that Mama had had tailored for her in Dublin. The dress was stylish, and Clara knew it suited her – Aunt Esther even said that the green of the velvet matched the colour of Clara's eyes. All around her the ladies were dressed in beautiful, and sometimes very elaborate, ball gowns, while the men were formally attired in ties and tails, with the occasional splash of colour where an officer wore the dress uniform of his regiment.

Food and drink had been laid on with abundance for the guests, and the rows of wine glasses and polished cutlery sparkled in the glow of the gas lamps. All the guests had arrived in horse-drawn carriages, which were lined up on the avenue outside, and the Parkinsons' hospitality extended to their drivers and footmen, who were given refreshments below stairs in the servants' dining area.

Musicians had been hired, and there would be dancing later, but for now the musicians played light classical pieces as the guests ate, drank and mingled. Clara could see that all of the Parkinson estate staff were dressed in new uniforms and looking their best, and she knew that this evening must be costing Papa a fortune. Aidan had asked her about the style of clothes that the staff and guests would wear, but Clara knew that other people would say it was wrong to spend all that money when there were poor people who were badly struggling. But not having the party wouldn't make their lot any better, Clara thought, and although she wished the world was fairer, she decided that for one night she wouldn't entertain any guilt and would simply enjoy the gathering.

Just then she heard a bell being rung, then Papa called for order as all of the guests assembled in the ballroom.

'Ladies and gentlemen, your forbearance, please, for a few moments,' he said. 'You're all very welcome here tonight. And as you know, it's traditional to subject you to performances from the Parkinson family – I'm afraid it's the price you have to pay for availing of our hospitality!'

There was laughter, then Clara watched as her father raised his hand in warning.

'I'm duty bound to inform you that the first performer tonight will be my good self,' he said. 'So those of you wishing to make a discreet escape may exit now through the same doors through which you entered!'

Again there was laughter, and Aunt Esther, who was standing behind Clara, whispered in her ear.

'He's really enjoying himself, isn't he?'

'In his element,' answered Clara with a grin.

'Looking forward to your own piece?'

'Yes, but a bit nervous too.'

'You'll be fine, you have that piece off to perfection.'

'How about you?'

'I want to savour tonight,' answered Esther. 'This time next year I'll be a married lady, so this is my last year performing as a Parkinson.'

'That's a bit sad, even though it's lovely that you're getting married.'

'Well, no sadness tonight,' answered Esther, 'and here's your papa going to cheer us all up.'

Clara could see that her father had joined the pianist who was going to accompany him, then he launched confidently into the newly popular Gilbert and Sullivan song, 'I Am the Very Model of a Modern Major General'.

It was a comedy song with complicated, clever lyrics, and Clara was impressed with how well her father carried it off. She realised that he must have rehearsed it in private, and when he finished there was loud applause and cries of 'Bravo!'

Her father bowed smilingly then addressed the gathering again.

'Thank you for your kindness in indulging me. And now, to raise the tone after my musical nonsense, may I present my daughter, Miss Clara Parkinson!'

Once again there was enthusiastic applause, and Clara felt her heart beginning to race as she bowed in acknowledgement then crossed the floor to collect her violin from beside the piano. She caught the eye of her mother, who nodded encouragingly. Clara removed the violin from its case, took a breath, then raised the instrument and tried to block out all thoughts of her audience. Instead she concentrated on the haunting melody as she played with feeling. The room had become utterly silent, and despite her resolve not to think about the audience, Clara was conscious that her playing was captivating the listeners. It was an intoxicating feeling, but Clara controlled it, concentrating on doing justice to the beauty of the piece. But even as she played, it was as if she were observing the scene from the outside, and she was aware that this was a moment she would never forget.

She began to approach the final bars of the composition and she relaxed a little, knowing that she had done herself justice and that she would be well received. Her listeners were still completely silent, lost in the music, when suddenly the silence was shattered by a deafening blast from outside.

Clara heard the sound of window panes shattering, and for an instant people were stunned into inaction. Then there were cries of alarm, and people began to scatter.

'It's a bomb!' someone called out, 'we're being attacked!'

'Don't panic!' cried Papa, 'Please. Stay calm. Don't stampede to the doors!'

Clara quickly placed her violin on top of the piano and looked about her. Despite her father's words there was chaos. But no further blast had followed the first one, so in fact it didn't seem to Clara as though the house was being attacked. Instead whatever the explosion had targeted was outside, and before she knew what she was doing, Clara found herself moving in the opposite direction to most people as she made for a small rear door at the far end of the ballroom.

In the mêlée she had lost sight of her parents and Aunt Esther, and she knew that if any of them saw her they would forbid her to go outside. *But they hadn't seen her. And she had to find out what was going on.*

Clara left behind the chaos of the ballroom and ran down a passage that led to a rear entrance to the kitchens. She raced to a side door that she knew opened to the outside and quickly pulled it open. Stepping outside, she heard the screaming of injured horses and she was hit by the acrid smell of smoke. Less than twenty yards away she could see carriage drivers running to where they had parked their carriages. She realised now that one of the carriages had been blown up, and she felt sickened to think of the suffering of the horses that had been maimed in the explosion.

She drew nearer to the scene of the carnage, horrified yet unable to stay away. 'Has anyone been killed – or hurt?' she asked a driver who was standing by the roadway looking dazed.

'No…doesn't look like it,' he answered shakily. 'We were…we were all inside gettin' fed.'

'Thank goodness for that!' said Clara. But she could hear the pitiful cries of wounded horses and it really upset her. 'Can we… can we get a vet for the horses?' she asked.

The driver looked uncomfortable. 'I'm sorry, Miss, but…they'll have to be put down.'

'That's…that's awful.' Clara looked about her. 'Who'd do something like this?'

'I don't know, Miss, but…well, the carriage blown to smithereens was Colonel Crawford's.'

Clara knew that Colonel Crawford was the landlord who had evicted the Horan family from their home at the end of October. And she realised, with a hollow feeling in her stomach, that tonight's attack was in retaliation. The Land War was getting worse – and it had just come, in no uncertain terms, to Ballydowd.

PART THREE

CONSEQUENCES

CHAPTER TWENTY-SEVEN

'Here she comes!' said Garrett, nudging his mother.

They were sitting in a pew in the sunlit interior of Ballydowd parish church, and Garrett felt his hopes rising as the sacristan approached with a sheet of paper in her hands. The woman had a satisfied look about her, and she even allowed herself a small smile as Garrett and his mother rose to meet her.

'I found what you wanted,' she said, 'I've written it out for you.'

'Thank you so much,' said Garrett.

'Yes, we really appreciate your help,' added Mam.

Ideally, Garrett would have liked to have gone with the sacristan and seen the original records relating to his ancestors. Mam, however, had pointed out that the parish administration was this woman's domain, and that she probably guarded her patch jealously.

'Now,' said the sacristan, reading her notes, 'Thomas Donnelly, baptised May the third, 1871. And the information you wanted; his father was a Timothy Donnelly, and his mother was Elizabeth Donnelly. The godparents were Seamus Cronin and Mary Ellen Maguire.'

'Brilliant,' said Garrett.

'Do you know,' said Mam, 'a thought has just struck me. We've been a bit male-oriented in our approach. Like, do we know the mother's maiden name?'

'Yes, actually,' said the sacristan, 'it was recorded on the baptismal certificate.' She consulted her notes again. 'It was Fitzgerald. She was originally Elizabeth Fitzgerald.'

'Great,' said Mam. 'We've been so caught up with Thomas Donnelly though, that it's only dawning on me now that we haven't tried to follow up on his wife's family.'

Garrett realised that this was true, but before he could respond the sacristan spoke.

'If you wanted me to look up the wife's family, you should have said so.'

'I'm sorry,' said Mam. 'We didn't really think it all through, did we, Garrett?'

'No, there were…there were so many strands to try and follow…'

'But now that we're in Ballydowd,' continued Mam, 'it strikes me Thomas may well have married a local girl. If he did there'd probably be a marriage certificate in your records.'

'And you want me to trawl through our records on the off-chance that they got married here?' said the sacristan.

Garrett wasn't sure what to make of the older woman. At first she had seemed a bit stiff, then she had seemed pleased to unearth the information they wanted, and now she seemed a little irked.

'I know you must think we're absolute pests,' said Mam with her most winning smile. 'And I realise a woman like yourself has lots of responsibilities. But we've come all the way from Dublin, so we'd be hugely grateful if we could find out a bit more about our ancestors. And women have tended to be written out of history. So as one woman to another, I think it would be good if we could do something here to redress that.'

Garrett realised that he could never have come up with a sales pitch like his mother had and he held his breath as the sacristan considered her answer. The woman's face gave nothing away, then eventually she nodded.

'All right,' she said. 'Tell me anything you know about her, or when they might have been married, and I'll have a look. But this is more of a long shot, and it could take a while.'

'Thanks a mill,' said Garrett. 'And we're not in a rush. We'll wait as long as it takes.'

CHAPTER TWENTY-EIGHT

Aidan threw a sod of turf onto the fire and watched as the sparks flew up the chimney of the abandoned cottage. Clara and Molly were poring over the sheet music of the French-Canadian song 'Alouette', and for a moment Aidan was alone with his thoughts. Today was the last day of 1880, and he felt a little unsettled as the New Year approached and he left behind the last turbulent weeks of December.

It was almost two weeks since the bombing at the Parkinsons' ball, and despite intense police activity no arrests had yet been made. Land League activists had been questioned vigorously – among them Uncle Sean – and their houses and farms searched, but to no avail. Aidan strongly suspected that Sean had been involved in the bombing of Colonel Crawford's carriage, and he reasoned that if Sean hadn't used up all the dynamite that night, then the rest must have been moved to a safer place.

Clara had been upset by the attack, and Aidan felt bad about that, yet he didn't feel he could inform on a member of his own family. He told himself that nobody had been killed or injured in the blast, and that he had no definite proof that Sean was involved, but he still felt a nagging unease. What would happen if in future someone *was* killed? Mr Quigley had taught them in religious instruction that it was a sin of omission to do nothing if that allowed evil to go ahead unchecked.

'A penny for your thoughts!' said Molly now, breaking his reverie.

'Sorry, I was…'

'Miles away?' suggested Clara.

Aidan nodded. 'I was just thinking about the future and…and the year we've had.'

'It's had its ups and downs all right,' said Clara, her tone more serious.

Aidan knew she was referring to the bombing, even though they had mostly succeeded in their arrangement of not letting the turmoil of the Land War impinge on their secret music sessions. The arrival of Clara's cousins from Norfolk had put an end to their get-togethers over Christmas. In anticipation of that, Clara had come up with a clever system of communication whereby messages were left behind a loose brick in the boundary wall of the Parkinson estate, which was how today's meeting had been organised.

They had previously agreed that it wouldn't be possible to exchange proper Christmas presents – their parents would have wanted to know the source – but they had belatedly given each other small tokens on meeting today, the first time since Christmas that Clara had been free of her cousins. Aidan had given Clara a miniature wooden horse that he had carefully carved, and Molly had given her an intricately embroidered handkerchief. Clara, in turn, had given each of them a small watercolour that she had painted. Aidan and Molly had already given each other gifts on Christmas Day, as they always did. But there was something special about today's exchange of secret gifts, and it felt to Aidan that the personal nature of the presents marked a cementing of their friendships, despite the growing conflict and its effect on their families.

'Still, 1880 wasn't all bad,' said Molly. 'We got to know each other.'

'For me that's been the best part of the whole year,' said Clara.

Aidan was touched by her sincerity. 'Thanks, Clara,' he said. 'You're…you're right, it's been great.'

'And here's hoping 1881 will be even better,' added Molly.

'Let's toast to that,' suggested Clara, taking up the bottle of homemade lemonade that she had brought along, and topping up their glasses.

Aidan desperately wanted to believe that next year *would* be better, but he wasn't sure. Mr Parnell, the leader of the Irish Party, had been arrested by the authorities three days previously, and there was no guarantee that the Bessborough Commission would give the farmers a fairer deal when they issued their report. But he tried to put his worries aside, and lifted his glass of slightly flat lemonade.

'To 1881,' said Clara.

Molly clinked glasses with her. 'To 1881.'

'To 1881, Aidan,' said Clara with a smile.

He clinked glasses and smiled back. 'Absolutely. To 1881.'

CHAPTER TWENTY-NINE

Molly watched the snowflakes swirling through the January sky as she and Aidan approached the schoolyard. It was only a light flurry, but Molly hoped that it might snow more heavily, like it had the previous winter, when she had enjoyed snowball fighting, makeshift tobogganing, the building of elaborate snowmen, and sliding on the frozen canal. Molly had an excellent sense of balance and could slide as fast as any of the boys. The Tobins had tried to discourage her by calling her a tomboy, but Molly believed that girls were as entitled as boys to be adventurous, and she had thoroughly enjoyed the sliding competitions on the ice.

The memory of that fun-filled time made her feel a little sad as she thought of how much things had changed. Only a year ago she had been popular and accepted at school, but the clashes between the Land League and the RIC meant that some pupils were now much cooler towards her. It hadn't got to the point where her family was being ostracised, and there were local people who recognised that her father was a decent man whose job placed him in a difficult position. But Molly still found it hurtful to be subtly excluded – and sometimes not so subtly – by pupils with whom she had once been friendly.

She entered the school yard, closely followed by Aidan. Iggy

Tobin noted their arrival and smirkingly called out. 'Here they are, Tweedledee and Tweedledum.'

Molly didn't expect anything but low-level hostility from the Tobin twins, but she was disappointed when some of the other pupils laughed at Iggy's remark. She knew that many of them were afraid of the Tobins, and that some had probably laughed to curry favour, but she still had to work to hide her disappointment.

'Don't mind him', said Aidan quietly.

'Tweedledee and Tweedledum is right,' said Peadar Tobin, stepping forward. 'But I've a question for you, Daly,' he said, looking aggressively at Aidan.

Molly stopped and stood in solidarity with him.

'Really?' said Aidan, injecting a hint of sarcasm into his voice.

'Yes, really. Your family are for the Land League, so why are you hanging around with the daughter of a traitor?'

'My father isn't a traitor!' said Molly.

'I wasn't talking to you, I was talking to him,' said Peadar aggressively.

'Before I answer your question,' said Aidan calmly, 'let me ask you a question. If your father murdered your mother, should they hang you?'

Peadar looked bemused. 'What?!'

'If your father killed your mother, would they hang you?'

'That's a stupid question! Of course they wouldn't hang me!'

'Because you're not responsible for what your father does,' said Aidan. 'Just like Molly's not responsible for what her father does.'

Molly felt a surge of affection for her friend. His argument had stumped Peadar, who couldn't come up with an immediate response. Instead his brother intervened.

'You think you're so smart, Daly,' said Iggy. 'But clever words won't put a roof over Jamsie Nolan's head when they evict him next week.'

Molly was taken aback, and she felt a sinking sensation in her stomach.

'Oh, didn't know that, did you not?' said Iggy.

Molly felt thrown and couldn't come up with a reply. She had thought that having his rent arrears paid for him would have allowed Jamsie Nolan to come up with his January rent. But clearly he hadn't, and the fund mustn't have been enough to support him for a second month running.

'Look at the shocked face on her!' said Iggy to his brother, before he turned back to Molly. 'Does your aul fella tell you nothing?' he asked.

The words hit home, and Molly felt angry. *Da should have told her – and not let her find out like this.* But she wouldn't show disloyalty in front of Iggy Tobin, and so she faced him. 'You don't know the first thing about my father,' she said.

'I know him and his cronies will beat the living daylights out of anyone who tries to stop the eviction.'

Molly remembered the cuts and bruises Da had played down after the Horan eviction, and she wondered if there was some truth in Iggy's claim. *Well, there was one way to find out.* She needed to know what happened at evictions. She was *entitled* to know, if it was going to be thrown at her in school. The solution was suddenly clear. She had to go and see for herself. Da would never give her permission, so she wouldn't ask for permission. She would be discreet, and make sure she wasn't seen, but her mind was made up – she was going to be there.

Just then the school bell rang. 'Let's go, Aidan,' she said, then she turned away from the Tobins and walked purposefully towards the classroom.

'Don't be angry with me, Mama.'

Clara's mother raised an eyebrow. 'Angry over what?'

Clara paused, trying to find the right words. They were seated before a blazing fire in the drawing room and had just been served afternoon tea by one of the servants. Outside the big bay window there was a dusting of snow, and Clara was looking forward to riding out on Shamrock later on, and savouring how the snow magically altered the appearance of the estate. First, though, she needed to talk about something that had started to bother her.

'I know it's awful about the explosion we had,' she said tentatively, 'and all the other trouble with the Land League, but…'

'But what, love?' prompted her mother.

'But I was thinking that a lot of that might never have happened, if things were a bit fairer.'

'You're not…you're not seriously suggesting, Clara, that planting a bomb is justified because a tenant is in dispute with his landlord?'

'No, of course not. But it says in the Bible to love your neighbour. How are you doing that if you evict a family onto the side of the road?'

'I grant you it's a difficult situation. But a landowner can't be responsible for the welfare of all his tenants' families.'

'Then what does loving your neighbour mean?'

'It means…it means trying not to harm anyone. Doing good when you can – within reason.'

'But…is that not being really easy on ourselves, Mama? It's not hard for us to love our neighbour when they're other landowners like us. And it's not hard for us to enjoy the life we have here. But is it fair?'

'It's how society is, Clara.'

'Yes, but with all due respect, Mama, that's not what I asked.'

'Sorry?'

'I asked is it fair?'

There was a long pause, and Clara hoped she hadn't gone too far.

'The world has never been fair,' answered her mother eventually, her tone surprisingly gentle. 'Since the time of Adam and Eve the world's been a flawed place, full of suffering and pain. In the next life all will be well, but in this life there are fortunate people – and there are unfortunates. We can't change all that, Clara. What

189

we can do is be kind when possible, and give thanks for our own good fortune.'

Clara sipped her tea and nibbled on a biscuit, unsure how to respond. All her life she had been used to being waited upon by servants, and to having fine food and clothes available as a matter of course. But her friendship with Aidan and Molly, and the protests of the Land League, had opened her eyes to the fact that her family's lifestyle was highly privileged – and that some of those privileges were at the expense of other people.

'The best thing we can do, Clara, is pray for a peaceful outcome, and for wisdom to prevail when the Commission makes its report.'

Clara thought that Mama was too comfortably inward-looking, but she didn't feel that she could say that. The wish for a peaceful outcome, however, was something she could support, and so she nodded, glad of a way out.

'I'll pray for peace then,' she said solemnly. 'I'll pray for it every night.'

Aidan felt deeply frustrated. In the three months since he had met Clara Parkinson he had managed to get away for their secret Sunday afternoon meetings unhindered, and without being detected. Today, though, his father had said that he needed Aidan's help, and Aidan had been unable to explain that he was meant to meet Clara and Molly. It would be another full week before they could have their next musical get-together, although in truth the music was now only part of the attraction, and the jokes, riddles, and growing friendship mattered as much as the tunes they played.

Ma was tidying up after their Sunday lunch of ham and cabbage. Normally Aidan's sister Brigid could have helped Da and Uncle Sean with the cutting and lettering of posters and placards that they were making to protest against the planned eviction of the Nolan family. Brigid, however, was gone, having started work this week in a big grocer's shop in Galway. Ma and Da had been in tears when she left, and Aidan too missed his sister's presence about the house. And now, in her absence, his free afternoon was going to be spent making placards and posters.

Da went off to get more wood for the placards, and when Ma finished tidying and said she was going to feed the hens, Aidan knew that this was his chance to question Uncle Sean. They hadn't been alone together since the night of the bombing, and Aidan felt a little nervous now as he tried to find the best way to raise the subject.

'Uncle Sean?' he said, taking a break from cutting cardboard rectangles for the placards.

'Yes?'

'Can I ask you something?'

Sean lowered the saw he had been using to trim the poles for the placards. 'Sure. What's on your mind?'

His tone was relaxed, but Aidan knew that could change.

'It's about the night of the bombing.'

'What about it?' said Sean, and sure enough, his voice now sounded wary.

'What would have happened if someone was killed?'

'No one was killed.'

'But they could have been.'

'It was done carefully. The guests and the drivers were all inside when it went off. So nobody was going to be killed.'

Aidan felt nervous. He couldn't admit to knowing about the dynamite from when he had searched Sean's farm, but he had to prod him a little. He forced himself to look his uncle in the eye. 'You seem to know a lot about it,' he said.

'And you *don't* need to know a lot about it. Or *anything* about it. It's better that way.'

'Better for who?'

'Better for you.'

Aidan felt a jolt of anger. Sean's response sounded like a threat, and he resented being spoken to like that in his own home. 'But not better for the people being bombed,' he retorted, 'or the horses blown to smithereens, or any passers-by who'd be killed if the timing went wrong.'

'The timing *wasn't* wrong. And horses are killed every day of the week in slaughterhouses. As for the people being bombed? We're talking about Colonel Crawford, who threw the Horans out of their home without a second thought. Do you think someone like Crawford would listen to reason? Or would ever take tenants' rights seriously before this? But I'll tell you something for nothing – he'll take us seriously now.'

'Us?'

'The Land League. Since his precious carriage was destroyed, Crawford knows he can't just do as he pleases. And that sends a message to other bullying landlords. And to the Bessborough Commission.'

Aidan realised that there was some truth in this, but he also felt there was a different kind of bullying involved in injuring cattle or planting a bomb. Before he could respond, Sean spoke again.

'Look, I know you've been friends with Molly O'Hara since you were tots. And it's not her fault that her family is RIC. But I'm sure she's been spouting whatever arguments she's heard at home, so it's important, Aidan – really important – that you don't let her poison your mind. This is war, a fight to the finish. And for the first time ever, our side is winning. Make certain you stay on the winning side. Do you understand?'

Aidan had all sorts of reservations about what Sean was saying, but his instinct told him to bide his time and not show his hand.

'Yes,' he answered slowly. 'Yes, I understand.'

CHAPTER THIRTY

Molly hid her school bag, sliding it in behind the door of a disused barn on the outskirts of town. She felt slightly guilty, never having played truant before, but she couldn't sit in a classroom this morning while the Nolan eviction took place just a couple of miles away.

Molly climbed over the gate at the edge of the field in which the barn stood, then regained the road and walked swiftly away. She hoped that she wouldn't bump into anyone when she should have been at school, but if she was questioned, she would claim to be delivering an urgent message to her father.

The light snow of the previous week had melted, but it was still a cold, blustery, January day. Molly quickened her pace, partly to keep warm, but also from a desire to get to the Nolan farmhouse in time to see what actually took place at evictions.

She followed the winding country road, her mind drifting back to yesterday. She had met Clara in the abandoned cottage, and with Aidan unavailable it was the first time that the two girls had spent time alone together. Although they had played some music, for most of the afternoon they had simply chatted. Molly had confided how worried she was about her father's role in today's eviction – both of the risk of him being injured, and regarding his role in making a family homeless.

194

Clara had been sympathetic on both counts, and had confided her own worries over what the future might hold. By the time the two girls parted, Molly knew that the bond between them had been deepened, and she was grateful once more that Aidan had brought them all together. Thinking about Aidan, she suspected that he would have wanted to accompany her today. But she hadn't told him her plans, not wanting to get him into trouble at school, or in danger at the eviction if things turned violent.

For herself, though, she would take whatever punishment might come her way in school, and risk whatever happened at Nolan's farm. *She simply had to see the eviction, and her father's role in it.* Picking up her pace further, she continued on her way.

Home-made flags fluttered in the chill wind and a large banner stating 'Hold onto your Land' was draped across the farmhouse roof as both Land League activists and local people supported Jamsie Nolan in resisting eviction. The chant 'no evictions!' had gone up, and as Molly watched from her hiding place in a ditch at the far side of the farmyard, she felt the hairs rise on the back of her neck. Whatever the rights and wrongs of the situation, there was something primitive and stirring about the roar of the large group gathered to support the Nolan family.

The farmhouse was occupied, the windows barricaded from the inside with wood, and Molly sensed that the charged atmosphere could easily lead to a violent clash. She could see her father with a group of RIC constables, their rifles slung over their shoulders and their faces grim. At least Da wasn't in command today, she thought, with a self-important inspector from Mullingar instead issuing orders to the policemen.

The RIC role was to support the sheriff's men, who would do the actual removal of goods from the Nolan homestead. Additionally, there was a unit of British soldiers on standby, their red tunics striking an incongruously colourful note in the bleak January surroundings.

Molly's eyes scanned the crowd. She picked out Aidan's father and uncle amongst the crowd of Land League supporters surrounding the cottage, many of whom carried placards that stated NO EVICTIONS. She desperately hoped that the showdown wouldn't descend into violence, and in particular that Da wouldn't end up in a physical confrontation with people who were his neighbours.

There were lots of women among the crowd, some of them quite elderly, and Molly realised that the whole local community in the Nolan's townland had turned out to try and halt the eviction. Suddenly there was a stirring among the crowd, and the chanting died down as the police inspector raised his hand and walked purposefully towards the line of protesters in front of the cottage. He paused, then spoke in a loud voice. 'James Nolan, I call upon you to exit peacefully the premises that you are unlawfully occupying.'

'You mean *his home*!' shouted a voice from the crowd.

There was cheering, which the inspector ignored. 'Mr Trevor Campbell is the lawful owner of this property,' he continued, 'and he's exercising his right to repossess it. Be assured that right will be upheld. If you leave now, no one will be hurt. If you resist, many people may be hurt, but the property will be occupied in the end. I call upon you to see sense and leave the property now.'

'He broke his back working this farm for twenty years!' shouted a voice from the crowd.

'And now his tenancy is over,' said the inspector. 'I'm not arguing further. Leave the premises, Mr Nolan, or I'll have no option but to force an entry.'

Molly held her breath, hoping that wouldn't happen. Then a voice called out from within the cottage. 'This is my home! If you want it, you'll have to take it!'

A cheer went up from the crowd, and they resumed the 'no evictions' chant.

The inspector stood unmoving for a moment, then he turned away and gestured to the sheriff's men. Molly saw them unloading a battering ram from one of their carts, and suddenly the atmosphere grew uglier with the chant being replaced with roars of protest.

Molly heard cries of 'traitors!' and 'lapdogs!' as the sheriff's men prepared the battering ram that would be used to smash in the front door.

The inspector turned to the assembled RIC men. 'Draw batons,' he ordered.

Molly felt her stomach tighten with fear as the policemen withdrew their wooden truncheons to a howl of protest. She could see her father standing stony-faced at the front of the line of constables. She thought that if he was scared, he was covering it well, but Molly could feel her own knees trembling.

'Clear a path to the door,' ordered the inspector.

The RIC men moved forward, and Molly hoped that at the last minute the protestors would step aside. Instead the chant of 'no evictions' started up again, louder than ever, and the protestors in the front line stood their ground.

The policemen were holding their heavy truncheons in a threatening fashion, but now the protestors who had been holding placards aloft lowered them, and gripped the wooden placard handles as weapons. For a moment there was a stand-off, then the inspector repeated his order.

'Clear a path!'

Molly looked on in despair as the police and protestors clashed, the scene descending into chaos within seconds. The chanting was replaced by screams and shouts as the constables batoned those blocking the path to the cottage. The protestors fought back fiercely, and Molly saw one policeman falling to the ground and another tumbling backwards with blood pouring down his face. She lost sight of her father in the commotion, but saw the officer commanding the British soldiers ordering his men to take up formation in the rear. She reckoned that the use of troops would be a last resort, but she could see that the tide of battle wasn't going the way of the RIC. By now there were blood-soaked protestors lying on the ground, but other policemen had been injured and they hadn't been able to force a way through to the cottage door.

Molly watched with horror as the inspector from Mullingar drew his pistol.

'Draw arms!' he shouted, 'draw arms!'

Surely he wouldn't order his men to shoot unarmed civilians, she thought. And if he did, would Da carry out such an order? But the scene was chaotic, and Molly feared that in the heat of the moment anything was possible. Some of the RIC men were grappling with opponents and couldn't unsling their rifles from their backs, but others did. Suddenly a volley of shots rang out, and Molly saw that the inspector had fired his pistol. It took her an instant to realise that he had fired into the air, but the shots created panic and his cry of 'lay down your clubs!' went largely unheard as people ran screaming in all directions. Molly got a glimpse of her father shouldering his rifle, before losing sight of him again.

Three more shots now rang out, this time from the direction of the cottage.

'They've shot a polisman!' she heard a woman cry, 'they've shot a polisman!'

Molly felt her blood run cold, and everything around her now seemed to happen in a daze.

'Aim weapons, but hold fire!' she heard the inspector shouting. 'Aim weapons, but hold fire!'

RIC constables were starting to move forward, their rifles trained on the now retreating crowd, but all Molly could think about was her father. Clearly the authorities had been prepared for trouble, because now she saw two of the sheriff's men running forward with a stretcher. *Please, God,* she thought, *let it not be Da who's been shot.* From the corner of her eye she saw the battering ram being brought forward as constables cleared a path through the chaos of the retreating crowd. The red-coated troops were deploying to throw a cordon around the whole area, but Molly hadn't spotted her father, and now she only had eyes for the activity around the stretcher.

She held her breath as the two sheriff's men lifted it, then came lumbering back with the stretcher containing the body of the bloodied constable. Up until this Molly had remained hidden at the ditch, but now all she cared about was the identity of the man who had been shot and she stood up to get a better view.

The sheriff's men lifted the stretcher up to place it on one of the carts, but still Molly couldn't make out who the victim was. Then she saw a sight that caused her heart to pound. Helping an injured constable back from the cottage was her father, upright and apparently uninjured. Molly felt a huge surge of relief. She was horrified that *anyone* had been shot, but she couldn't help but feel relieved that the victim wasn't Da. Overwhelmed by her emotions, she felt her eyes well up with tears. She sat dazedly on a stone wall by the edge of the ditch, as the sheriff's men swung the battering ram, and smashed in the front door of the cottage.

There were screams and roars as the RIC stormed inside, then Molly watched as Jamsie Nolan was swiftly dragged from his home, his wife pleading with the constables not to hurt him. Jamsie was a small, slight man, and Molly couldn't help but feel sorry for him as he was manhandled away by two heavily built policemen. Jamsie's wife turned back to the door to comfort four frightened-looking children who had followed her out. All of them were badly-dressed, and the youngest two were barefoot. The smallest child was clutching a tattered rag doll and sobbing uncontrollably, and Molly watched as her mother tried to comfort her.

Within seconds the sheriff's men began to emerge from the cottage, carrying the family's few pieces of furniture and throwing them in a heap at the side of the roadway. It seemed to Molly like the final indignity for a family that was being left without shelter on a winter night, and she turned away, unable to bear what she was seeing. The relief Molly had felt at Da's safe-keeping, coupled with the horror of what she had just witnessed, was too much for her, and the tears that had been welling up in her eyes now ran freely down her cheeks, as she sat unmoving on the cold stone wall.

CHAPTER THIRTY-ONE

'What's going on, do you reckon?' Garrett was sitting with his mother in the sunlit silence of Ballydowd parish church, but over twenty minutes had passed and there was no sign of the sacristan returning.

'I think she must have found something,' said Mam.

'Yeah?'

'If she'd drawn a complete blank she would have been back by now.'

Garrett felt a slight stirring of excitement. He was already pleased to have gained more information about Thomas Donnelly. But Mam had been right, and in his focus on tracking down his great-great-grandfather he had overlooked exploring the family line of his great-great-grandmother. Before he could muse over it any further he saw a movement from the corner of his eye and he swung around to see the sacristan approaching. Once again she had a sheet of paper in her hands, and despite having cautioned himself not to expect too much, Garrett felt his hopes rising.

'Sorry for keeping you,' said the sacristan.

'Not at all,' said Mam.

'But I found what I was looking for – and a bit more.'

'Brilliant.' said Garrett.

'Your hunch was good,' continued the woman, 'Thomas Donnelly married a local woman, Helen O'Hara. Their wedding day was May the twenty-third, 1898, here in this church.'

'Wow,' said Mam. 'Just imagine, if they hadn't done that we wouldn't be here today. We wouldn't even exist!'

'I hadn't thought of it like that,' said Garrett.

'And you said you had more information?' said Mam, turning to the other woman.

The sacristan nodded. 'When I found the marriage certificate I got the bit between my teeth, so I looked at burial records for her family.'

'And you found something?' said Garrett.

The sacristan paused, and Garrett saw that she was enjoying the drama of her revelation.

'I did indeed. They have a family plot – and it's only about thirty yards from where we're standing now'

'They're buried here? In the church grounds?' asked Mam.

'Yes, in the graveyard to the rear of the chapel. I've noted the plot number.' She looked at Garrett. 'Would you like to see the grave?'

'Yes, please, I'd love to.'

'All right,' said the sacristan. 'Follow me.'

CHAPTER THIRTY-TWO

Aidan couldn't keep his mind on his prayers. He was kneeling beside his father on the flagstones in front of the turf fire in the kitchen, as his mother led the three of them in saying the rosary. It was a long prayer that the family didn't normally pray, but this wasn't a normal week. It was just three days since the eviction, and only a day since the funeral of Edward Moynihan, the RIC man who had been shot.

Aidan was glad that despite their Land League sympathies his parents had included the dead policeman in tonight's prayers. Primarily though, they were praying for Pat Brennan, the hot-headed activist who had been caught with a handgun and arrested for the shooting. The authorities had moved at speed – presumably to send out a message to others – and Brennan had been convicted and was sentenced to be hanged next week. An appeal had been lodged against the death sentence, and it was for the success of the appeal that the family was praying now.

Aidan found himself torn. Pat Brennan was only in his mid-twenties, and it seemed an awful waste that such a young life should be snuffed out. But on the other hand Edward Moynihan had been just thirty-two when Brennan had ended his life. Aidan knew that Uncle Sean would argue that the authorities used force, and that the Land League had to meet that with force of its own. But that approach could lead to an endless cycle of tit-for-tat violence, and Aidan felt that peaceful protest and boycotting were better tactics.

Ma was finishing up the rosary now and she added one final intention to their prayers.

'Lord, look with favour on our pleas,' she said, 'and guide the Bessborough Commission to reach a speedy and a just conclusion.'

Aidan suspected that Ma hadn't come up with that wording on her own, but he agreed with the thrust of it, and he joined his father in saying a heartfelt amen. They all rose from their knees, and Ma indicated the three chairs that were facing the fire.

'Sit down, let ye, and I'll make a sup of tea,' she said.

'Don't mind if I do,' answered Da, lowering himself into his usual chair to the right of the fire.

Aidan sat opposite him and he looked enquiringly at his father. 'Do you think…do you think Da, that praying for things really makes them happen?'

'Yes, son, I do. If enough of us pray for Pat Brennan, he might be spared. And if enough of us pray about the Commission, they might do the right thing as well. And you know what that could lead to eventually?'

'What?'

'You owning the farm here.'

'I don't…I don't want to own the farm,' said Aidan. He had been waiting a long time for the right moment to say it, but now, somehow, it had just come out.

'You don't want to own the farm?' said Da, his expression confused.

Aidan could see that Ma had stopped making the tea, and that she too looked surprised. But he had finally revealed his secret and he knew he mustn't back down now.

'No, Da. I'm sorry but that's not…it's not for me.'

'Why not?'

'Because…well, I'm not you. I know you like farming, Da, and that you'd love to own your own land, but…I'm different. I mean, you never asked me what *I* wanted.'

'I didn't think I had to. Our family have always been farmers.'

'And that's fine, for people who want it. But, Da…I don't mean to be rude…but…I don't want it.'

'So what *do* you want, love?' asked Ma.

Aidan hesitated, then spoke as confidently as he could. 'I want to work in a big city store. Selling clothes.'

'Clothes?' said his father.

'It's not a dirty word, Da. You wear clothes, don't you?'

'Everyone wears them – that's a stupid argument!'

'Larry,' said Ma gently, 'go easy.'

Aidan watched as his father breathed out, then raised his hands in acknowledgement of Ma's intervention. But he still looked badly taken aback, and Aidan spoke as persuasively as he could. 'Everyone wears clothes, Da. But someone has to make them, someone had to design them, someone has to sell them. They're real jobs, and that's the kind of work I'd love to do.'

'So all the battles fought by the Land League, all the progress we might make – it will count for nothing. You'd turn your back on the land.'

'No, Da. The fight is for freedom. Not to be evicted, to have a fair rent, to buy the land eventually if you choose. Freedom is having a choice. So please, Da – and Ma – when the time comes, let me choose. Otherwise…'

'Otherwise what?' said Da.

Aidan kept his voice respectful, but looked his father straight in the eye. 'Otherwise what on earth have we been fighting for?'

CHAPTER THIRTY-THREE

Clara urged her pony from a trot to a canter, confidently using the reins to guide Shamrock as she rode out across the Parkinson estate. The late afternoon sun was low in the sky and it bathed the landscape in a golden glow that belied the sharp nip in the air. Clara, however, didn't mind the cold when she was on horseback, and unless the weather was very bad she rode out most afternoons. With so much else in turmoil it was reassuring to have a routine, and the combination of fresh air and exercise usually lifted her spirits.

It was four days now since the eviction, and Clara had found it hard to get it out of her thoughts. Last night she had had a nightmare about the forthcoming execution of the Land League activist who had killed the policeman. But in her dream it was Clara who somehow found herself on the scaffold, while Jamsie Nolan, the evicted farmer, played the role of the executioner.

Dreams usually made little sense, but Clara knew that this one was triggered by guilt. Even though there was nothing she could do about it, Clara felt bad about being warm and cosy each night in bed, while the homeless Nolan family was at best taken in by relatives who didn't have the room, and at worst sheltering in a barn or stable.

Right now though, Clara concentrated on riding her pony and

on savouring the sounds and smells of the countryside as Shamrock cantered eagerly ahead. They rounded a bend in the track, then Clara abruptly reined in the pony.

'Whoa, boy, whoa,' she cried.

A man was lying injured on the ground, his riderless horse standing beside him.

Clara quickly dismounted and bent towards him. Part of her wondered what a stranger was doing on their land and on such a remote corner of the estate, but before she could think about it any further she realised that something was strange. The man was lying face down, but where the back of his neck should have been visible there was instead a blank white cloth. Clara dropped to her knees and reached out to him. Just as she did the man suddenly sprang to life and shot upright, grabbing Clara by the arms and spinning her around. The shock of his sudden gesture gave her a fright, but more disturbing was that fact that he was wearing a mask. Clara realised that it was actually a pillow case, with holes cut for the eyes, nose, and mouth, but before she could react, the man spoke.

'If you scream, I'll blow your brains out! Don't scream!'

Clara hadn't seen any gun, but she nodded vigorously. 'All right!' she said, 'all right!'

The man had risen fully now and he pushed Clara down onto the ground. He pulled her hands behind her back, then clamped them together with what she realised must be handcuffs. A surge of terror swept through her, but as if reading her thoughts, the man spoke reassuringly.

'You're not going to be hurt. Just do what you're told and all will be well.' From the corner of her eye Clara saw a horse and cart approaching and other masked men jumping down from it.

'I'm going to put a hood on you now, but I'll take off the hood and the handcuffs when we get where we're going.'

'No, please!' cried Clara, but she had barely said the words when the man pulled a small sack down over her head. Everything went dark, and the sack had a musty smell, but Clara tried not to panic. The first man lifted her to her feet, then one of the other men took her other arm and they guided her up and into the cart.

'Lie on the floor!' ordered the first man, and Clara did as she was told, her pulses racing madly. The hood was disorienting, and she felt even more claustrophobic when a heavy blanket was used to cover her up.

'OK, let's go!' cried the second man.

The cart took off, and Clara found herself being jolted as they went along the bumpy track. She tried to grapple with her fear, and told herself that thinking clearly could be of vital importance. It was terrifying to have been kidnapped, but so far the men hadn't been violent or abusive. And if it was money they were after, she knew that Papa was a wealthy man and that he loved her dearly. If it came to paying a ransom, her father wouldn't be found wanting, she felt sure.

Meanwhile she needed to keep her wits about her, and to work out where they were going. She felt a bump as they went out one of the rear exits of the estate and reached the public road, and she tried to keep tabs on the direction they were taking as the cart rattled on. It was difficult with the mask blocking the light, but she knew they had crossed over the Royal Canal when the cart ascended and descended a humpback bridge. They travelled on for what seemed an age, and eventually Clara became completely disoriented. Of course they could be deliberating bringing her round in circles, she told herself, and it was possible that their final destination might not be as far from home as it seemed.

The men never said another word, but finally the horse slowed down, and Clara reckoned that they had pulled into a farmyard. She felt the blanket being lifted off her, then she was helped to her feet and down off the cart.

'Nearly there now,' said the first man as he took her arm and she gingerly walked across the stone flags of a farmyard. She heard what sounded like the door of a barn being opened, then the man guided her inside.

Clara felt the hood being lifted off her head and she breathed in deeply, relieved to be free from the musty smell of the sack. She saw that she was in a sturdy barn full of hay, and that her captor was a tall man who still wore his pillowcase mask. True to his word, he reached behind her and freed her from the handcuffs. Clara immediately felt more herself now that she was unshackled and could see. Her instinct told her not to behave like a victim, and she drew herself up to her full height and spoke as steadily as she could. 'What's going on?' she demanded.

'Don't worry, we won't mistreat you.'

'Why am I here?'

The man hesitated, then seemed to reach a decision. 'I suppose you're entitled to know. You're a bargaining chip.'

'A bargaining chip?'

'Even someone as pampered as you must know there's a land war. And now you're a part of it. If the powers-that-be see sense, all will be well, and you'll be released.'

'And...if all doesn't go well?'

The man hesitated again. 'We'll cross that bridge if we come to it,' he said. Without another word he turned abruptly away and left the barn, locking the door behind him.

Clara stood unmoving. The unspoken threat in the man's words had been chilling, and she bit her lips, trying hard to keep her tears at bay.

CHAPTER THIRTY-FOUR

Molly had never been particularly religious, but she prayed now like she had never prayed before. She still found it hard to believe that her friend had been kidnapped yesterday afternoon, and there was a sense of shock among this morning's congregation at Sunday Mass. What made it even harder for Molly was the fact that nobody except Aidan knew that she was friends with Clara. She was hoping to get some time alone with Aidan after Mass ended, but meantime she had no one with whom she could share the fears that had kept her awake for a long time last night.

Father Fitzgibbon, the parish priest, had said at the start of the service that today's mass would be for the repose of the soul of the deceased constable, Edward Moynihan. He had also asked the congregation to pray for a just and merciful outcome to the appeal for Pat Brennan, and for the safe, speedy return of Clara Parkinson to her family – about which he would have more to say in his sermon.

Molly thought it sounded like he was hedging his bets and trying to appease everyone. In a way she could understand that, as a definite split had emerged in what had once been a united community. Her own father, who sat between her sister Helen and Mam, had a cut hand and bruised cheek from the violent clashes at the eviction, and some of their neighbours were now very clearly ostracising the family. Feelings were running high too at the proposed execution of Pat Brennan, although many people were also appalled at the killing of Constable Moynihan and the abduction of Clara.

Normally Molly liked the atmosphere at Sunday Mass, especially when, like today, the sunlight streamed in through the stained-glass windows and the air was scented with candle wax and the faint aroma of incense. This morning, though, she was too disturbed to take in her surroundings, and instead she kept her eyes closed and prayed fervently that Clara was safe and that she wasn't being mistreated.

The priest had been saying the mass in Latin, but now Molly became aware that his sing-song delivery had ceased. She opened her eyes to see that Father Fitzgibbon was mounting the pulpit. He was an overweight man of about sixty, and as he slowly climbed the steps of the pulpit, Molly sat up expectantly. The priest's sermons were unpredictable, sometimes thought-provoking, at other times too meandering. Today, though, he was going to address the life-threatening events taking place in the parish, and Molly hoped that he would have the nerve to say what was needed – even if that made him unpopular with some of his parishioners.

'In the name of the Father, and the Son, and the Holy Ghost,' said the priest, and Molly and the rest of the congregation blessed themselves and waited for him to begin.

Molly could see that almost everyone she knew in the village was present. Mr Quigley was seated in the front row, and all of her classmates and their families were scattered throughout the church, including the Tobins in their usual place at the back. Aidan was there with his parents, although his uncle, who sometimes attended mass with the Dalys, was missing.

'This has been a very troubling week in our parish,' said Father Fitzgibbon. 'There's already been one death with the killing of Constable Edward Moynihan, and whatever our views of the rights and wrongs of the land issue, the taking of a human life is nothing short of tragic. Likewise, there is the case of Patrick Brennan, for whom we've prayed today. His situation is one we can't control, and we leave his fate in the loving and ever-merciful hands of the Lord.

'But there is another case that may be within the control of some. I refer to the kidnapping of Miss Clara Parkinson yesterday afternoon. To abduct a child from her home is an appalling act. Relations between our community and the Parkinson family have traditionally been good, but even those who feel strongly that Mr Parkinson is on the opposing side on the land issue, must recognise that his child is an innocent party, and her kidnapping is a totally immoral act.'

Molly subtly glanced around her, but found it hard to gauge how the congregation was taking Father Fitzgibbon's approach. There was absolute silence, with none of the usual coughing and fidgeting that happened during sermons, but most people's expressions were impassive, and it was impossible to tell what they thought.

'The idea of threatening the life of a child to blackmail the authorities is an evil and indeed seriously sinful act,' said the priest.

Molly swallowed hard. At the back of her mind she had feared that this was probably why Clara had been kidnapped, but Da had refused to discuss it at home, and to hear Father Fitzgibbon say it bluntly was disturbing.

'If members of this congregation have any knowledge of what has happened to Miss Parkinson, or who her abductors are, they are duty bound, as practising Catholics, to reveal that knowledge,' continued the priest. 'And if anyone doesn't wish to contact the authorities directly, they may come to me in strict confidence. Now, I know there's long been a tradition in Irish life of despising the informer. But as your parish priest let me tell you that most definitely, that does not apply here. A truly evil deed has been done in Ballydowd, and anyone with any involvement in this kid-napping must, *absolutely must*, bring it to an end now. Both for the welfare of their immortal soul, and to save the life of an innocent child.' Fr Fitzgibbon paused for effect, then slowly blessed himself. 'In the name of the Father, and of the Son, and of the Holy Ghost, amen.'

Molly blessed herself with the rest of the congregation. She admired the priest for taking such a firm stand, and she hoped and prayed that what he had done might save her friend.

Aidan sat uncomfortably on a log in the dell where he had

arranged to see Molly. But although their meeting place was less cosy than the abandoned cottage, Aidan's discomfort had little to do with the cool January air, and more to do with his troubled mind. He hadn't had a chance to talk properly to Molly immediately after Mass, and now, a couple of hours later, he still wasn't sure what he was going to say to her.

She approached, and they exchanged low-key greetings, then Molly sat on the other end of the log. They had agreed previously to forget about playing music this afternoon, and Molly got straight to the heart of the matter.

'What do you think will happen to Clara?'

'Nothing, I hope.'

'That's it though. We're just hoping.'

'Hoping and praying.'

'Yes. But...I wish there was something we could actually do.'

Aidan paused, then came to a decision. 'Maybe there is,' he said.

'How do you mean?'

'I'm going to tell you some things, Molly. But first...first I need you to promise me you won't tell anyone.'

'All right.'

'Not the priest in Confession, not your mother – and especially not your da. Promise?'

'I've already promised, Aidan. What's the big secret?'

Aidan took a deep breath, then spoke quietly even though there was no one in sight. 'I think...I think it's possible my Uncle Sean was involved in kidnapping Molly.'

'What?'

'I know it sounds awful, but...he's fanatical about the Land League. I think he was involved in blowing up Colonel Crawford's carriage.'

'What makes you think that?'

'I searched his farm last month, when he wasn't there. And I found...I found sticks of dynamite.'

'Oh God, no!' said Molly, her hand going to her mouth.

'I've no proof that was the dynamite that blew up the carriage. And the police found nothing when they did searches after the bombing. But I think there's a strong chance he was involved.'

Aidan could see that he had shocked his friend, but now she looked him squarely in the eye.

'Do you really think he'd do that? Kidnap an innocent girl?'

Aidan hesitated but forced himself to be honest. 'He might, if he thought a man's life was at stake. And Pat Brennan's life *is* on the line.'

'And would he...could you see him hurting Clara?'

'I don't want to believe he'd do that. I really don't. Taking her could just be a tactic, a bluff.'

'Let's hope so. I...I couldn't bear to think...'

'I know,' said Aidan. 'Neither could I.'

'The dynamite is a link to the carriage bombing. Is there anything linking your uncle to kidnapping Clara?'

'I've no proof,' answered Aidan. 'But he's obsessed with the Land League, and I reckon he *was* involved in the bombing. It would be some coincidence if another big crime was committed, and he had nothing to do with it.'

Molly seemed to consider this. 'Yes,' she said. 'I suppose it would.'

Aidan had wanted to hear his friend's opinion, but now that she had endorsed his suspicions it made things feel frighteningly real.

'Father Fitzgibbon says anyone who knows anything must speak up,' said Molly.

'And I will. But not to Father Fitzgibbon.'

'To who then?'

'To my uncle. The more I think about it, the more obvious it is. I'll go to his cottage now, and if he's out I'll search it from top to bottom for clues.'

'And if he *is* there?'

'Then I'll have it out with him.'

'That's...that's very brave, Aidan.'

'Clara is our friend. I can't just stand by.'

Molly looked thoughtful. 'Actually...neither can I. She's my friend too, Aidan, so...'

'What?'

Molly looked him in the eye. 'Let me in on this. Whatever needs doing, let's do it together.'

CHAPTER THIRTY-FIVE

Garrett excitedly took out his mobile phone and activated camera mode as he followed his mother and the sacristan through the graveyard behind Ballydowd Church. The air was filled with birdsong, and Garrett looked forward to seeing the resting place of his ancestors from one hundred and fifty years ago, and photographing the details on the headstone.

'That's the grave, there,' said the sacristan, coming to a halt. 'I'll leave you to it.'

'Thanks a million,' said Garrett.

'Yes, many thanks for all your help,' added Mam.

'You're welcome.'

The sacristan moved off, and Garrett looked at the headstone. It was a granite slab, weathered by time, but the lettering was still quite clear, and he studied it closely, then took some pictures.

'Do you see what I see?' said Mam after a moment.

'What?'

'Look at the date of the births, and the date of the deaths. Anything strike you?'

'Eh…yes, actually. One death seems very early.'

'That's what I thought too. I'd love to find out what happened there.'

Garrett looked at his mother. 'Me too. It's like every time

we seem to be reaching the end, something new crops up.'

'Yeah. But now that it has, it's hard to walk away.'

'So…what's our next move?' asked Garrett.

His mother looked thoughtful. 'I have an idea. It might lead nowhere, but it could pay off.'

'OK,' he said. 'What's the idea?'

CHAPTER THIRTY-SIX

Clara was determined not to act like a victim. The barn in which she was being held prisoner had two small windows high in the wall and was locked from the outside, but that didn't necessarily mean that escape was impossible. It was midday on Sunday now, and bright sunlight was shining through the windows. The barn was filled with stacks of hay, and Clara was moving the hay and working her way along the bottom of the wall, feeling to see if there were any loose planks of wood that she might be able to prise away.

So far, her captors had treated her well. Last night they had provided her with blankets, a pillow, and a candle, as well as a large jug of water and a plate of hot stew, and this morning they had brought her porridge and brown bread. Despite her fear when their leader had suggested that she was a bargaining chip, Clara had consoled herself that the men wearing masks was a positive sign, suggesting they didn't want her giving descriptions of them when she was eventually released. It was still frightening being a prisoner, and last night Clara had given way to despondency, wishing she was safely home with Mama and Papa. She worried too about what had happened to Shamrock, and hoped he was all right. She had cried for a while, before pulling herself together, telling herself that she had to stay strong. After the shock of her abduction began to wear off, she found herself getting angry. She knew her parents would be worried sick, and she had been deprived of her liberty and frightened for her life. *She had to find some way to fight back.*

Marshalling her thoughts, she had decided to analyse everything that happened, both to give herself the best hope of escaping, and to be able to give evidence later on to bring her captors to justice. Although she hadn't seen their faces she recognised their accents as being local, and while they hadn't spoken a lot, she reckoned from their vocabulary that they weren't well educated. As for location, she calculated that they had travelled in the cart for perhaps an hour. That meant that she could be anywhere within about a ten-mile radius of home – which made for a large area. Wherever the barn was, Clara reckoned it was remote, as she hadn't heard any church bells in the distance, despite it being a Sunday morning.

Now she continued moving hay and feeling the base of the barn wall. So far all of the planking was secure, but Clara was determined to work her way around the whole barn in the hope of finding a weak spot. She carried on, then felt something hard in the hay. She quickly dug deeper, then uncovered a small wooden chest. Clara examined it closely and realised that it wasn't something old and long-abandoned. Instead the chest looked in good condition, and Clara felt her pulses starting to race a little. Whatever the chest contained, someone wanted it hidden. Clearly her captors hadn't allowed for Clara working her way along the base of the wall under the hay, and they thought their hiding place was secure. *But what could be in the chest?* Clara tried to open the clasp, but it wouldn't lift, and she saw that a key was required to open the lock. Before she could think about it any further Clara heard someone at the barn door, and she quickly replaced the chest and covered it with hay, then moved swiftly to another part of the barn as the door swung open.

'All right?' said the tall man, whom Clara had identified as the leader of the gang. He was wearing his mask as usual and was carrying food on a tray.

'Yes,' she answered, having decided that being courteous to her captors would improve the likelihood of interaction, and the chances for gaining information on them.

'I've brought you some lunch,' said the man, laying down the tray on of one of the bales of hay.

Clara could see that he had provided a bowl of soup, a cup of milk, and a plate with a slice of soda bread. 'Thank you,' she said.

'I need something from you.'

'Oh?'

'I see you have a monogrammed handkerchief,' he said, indicating where Clara had set it down on top of her pillow. 'They want proof that we have you, so we'll send that on.' he said holding out his hand.

Clara crossed to the pillow, took up the handkerchief, and handed it over.

'What are you demanding for my release?' she asked, trying to keep her voice strong.

'That they grant the appeal and don't hang Pat Brennan.'

'And if they grant that, you'll let me go?'

'We will. We'll blindfold you and drop you off somewhere miles from here.'

'Supposing he gets a long jail sentence?'

'He'll serve it like a man, and we'll still let you go.'

Clara was afraid to ask the next question, but she knew that she had to. 'And what…what happens if they don't grant the appeal?'

The man didn't answer at once, and Clara could feel her stomach fluttering. She wished she could see his face, but the mask meant she had no clue to his thinking.

'When they get this,' he said indicating the handkerchief, 'they'll know what's at stake – and they *will* grant the appeal.'

Without another word he turned on his heel and made for the door. Clara stood unmoving, trying to come to terms with what had been said, as her captor closed the door and locked it noisily behind him.

Molly felt her heart starting to thump as she approached a sharp bend in the narrow country road. She was accompanying Aidan for the showdown with his Uncle Sean, and she knew that his uncle's farm was around the next bend.

They were both still shocked by Clara's kidnapping, and Molly had bitterly criticised the Land League. Aidan however had argued that kidnapping children wasn't Land League policy, and that the people who had taken Clara were probably extremists acting off their own bat.

'Maybe so,' Molly had said. 'But it's handy for the Land League if someone else does the dirty work. They can disapprove, but still get their way and not have their man executed.'

'And what, the government don't want to have it both ways too? Condemn violence when the Land League does it, but unleash the RIC and the army when it suits them?'

Molly hadn't really thought of it that way before, but before she could respond, Aidan held up his hand.

'Let's not argue about who's in the wrong. We need to concentrate on Clara.'

'You're right,' conceded Molly. 'So, what do we do when we reach your uncle's farm?'

'If he's not there we'll search it together. See if we can find any clues, anything incriminating.'

'And if he is there?

'Let me try talking to him. On my own to begin with. All right?'

'All right.'

That had been twenty minutes ago, and now Molly and Aidan rounded the bend and cautiously approached the cottage. Molly could feel her stomach tightening with tension knowing that a confrontation might be just ahead. She found herself half-hoping that Aidan's scary uncle wouldn't be home, but then she thought of her kidnapped friend, and she steeled herself to be braver. 'No smoke from the chimney,' she observed.

'No. Doesn't guarantee he's not there though. Sometimes he's lazy and doesn't bother with a fire.'

'Right.'

'Why don't you hide in the bushes while I knock on the front door?' whispered Aidan as they drew nearer.

'Fine,' answered Molly, then she slipped into the heavy foliage of a clump of bushes at the gable end of the cottage.

Aidan approached the door and gave four loud knocks. On getting no reply, he knocked loudly again. When a third series of knocks got no response, Molly stepped out of the bushes, and Aidan rejoined her.

'Pity he's not here,' he said. 'But let's use the chance to search the place. Come on around the back.'

Molly followed him as he led the way to some outhouses. 'I thought you said he doesn't lock the back door?' she said. 'Are we not searching the cottage?'

'We will. But first I want to check out here. It's where I found the dynamite and the handcuffs.'

'Hidden in the chicken feed?'

'Yes. And now,' said Aidan stopping at the entrance to one of the outhouses, 'now the sacks are gone.'

'I suppose if your uncle *was* involved, he'd have moved any unused dynamite to somewhere else,' said Molly.

Aidan nodded. 'And if you were kidnapping someone, you'd

want to take the handcuffs to where that was happening, wouldn't you?'

'So, what do we do next?'

'Search the cottage from top to bottom.'

Molly had a vision of Aidan's uncle coming back and catching them, but she forced her fears aside. *She had to do whatever it took to free Clara.* 'Fine,' she said, 'top to bottom.'

CHAPTER THIRTY-SEVEN

'**I** want everyone on their very best behaviour,' said Mr Quigley, his tone unusually severe as he addressed the class. Strong January sunlight warmed the schoolroom, but the brightness of the morning contrasted with the teacher's sombre mood. 'The Parkinson family has been dealt a cruel blow with this kidnapping,' he said, 'and you'll pay them the courtesy of your full attention. I'm going out to escort them in now, and when Mr Parkinson speaks to you, I expect to be able to hear a pin drop. Understood?'

'Yes, sir,' answered the class.

'Very well. And not a peep out of you while I'm gone,' he added, before making for the classroom door.

'*The Parkinson family has been dealt a cruel blow*', mimicked Iggy Tobin softly.

'Pity about them!' said his brother, Peadar.

Aidan normally tried to avoid conflict with the twins, but today their casual nastiness caused something in him to snap, and he turned in his desk to face them. 'Do you think just once in your life you could have a bit of decency?'

'What's it to you, Daly?' said Iggy.

'Yeah, what's it to any of us if some stuck-up girl is missing?' said Peadar.

Aidan wanted to say that Clara wasn't stuck up at all, but he knew it would be disastrous to reveal his link to her. 'She's a human being just like us,' he said. 'And her family must be worried sick – just like *your* family would be, if *you* were missing.'

The twins didn't reply, and Aidan felt that he had won a small victory. Not much else though had gone his way since yesterday afternoon's visit to Sean's cottage. He and Molly had carefully searched the outhouses and barn, and then the rooms of the cottage without finding anything of interest. They had waited for several hours in the hope that Sean would return, but eventually they had been forced to return to their homes empty-handed.

Before he could think about it any further the classroom door now opened, and Mr Quigley ushered in the Parkinsons. Aidan could immediately see the strain on the faces of Mr and Mrs Parkinson, who were accompanied by a younger woman whom he knew to be Clara's Aunt Esther. The three of them were soberly dressed in what Aidan reckoned to be expensively tailored clothes, and Mr Quigley escorted the two ladies to chairs that had been laid out in readiness, with Mr Parkinson remaining standing.

'Despite the terrible circumstances,' said the teacher, 'it's an honour to welcome Mr and Mrs Parkinson, and Miss Parkinson, to our school today. Mr Parkinson wishes to address each class in person, and I know you'll listen attentively to what he has to say.'

Aidan watched, fascinated, as Mr Parkinson seemed to gather himself. Any time Aidan had seen him before he had looked like a commanding figure, a former officer who still carried himself with a solid sense of assurance. Aidan had always admired his impeccable dress sense, and had even questioned Clara about where her father had his clothes tailored. Today though there was a hint of vulnerability about Mr Parkinson as he stepped forward to speak.

'Thank you, Mr Quigley,' he said.

Aidan noted that he had the same sort of Anglo-Irish accent as Clara, and he spoke quietly, but with conviction.

'There can't be anyone in this room,' he said 'who doesn't know there's a bitter land war taking place. And some of us have found ourselves on different sides. But I'm asking you to overlook that, because I'm not here today as a land-owner. I'm here today as a father. A father whose beloved daughter – a girl who's just twelve years old – has been taken. I shudder to think what's going through her young mind these last two days. Whatever dispute is going on between landowners and the Land League has nothing to do with her. And I'm appealing…I'm appealing from the bottom of my heart that if anyone here knows anything – the slightest thing that might shed light on where she is, or who has taken her – I would ask you to come forward. As has already been said, it's not necessary to go to the police. You can approach Father Fitzgibbon in strict confidence, and he'll take the necessary steps. There will be no action taken against anyone for not coming forward sooner, but rather my heartfelt thanks, and that of my family. Please, don't let an innocent girl suffer. If you know anything – anything at all – please, do the right thing. Thank you.'

Aidan was touched by the sincerity of the speech, but now to his surprise Mrs Parkinson rose and stepped forward.

'I'd just like to add something,' she said.

'Of course,' agreed Mr Quigley.

Mrs Parkinson looked around the classroom, making eye contact with the students, then she spoke softly, 'Clara is my only child. Imagine how your mothers would feel if one of you was abducted. Imagine how you'd feel if your sister suddenly was taken from you. Well, my girl, my child, the love of my life, has been taken. If anyone knows anything, I'm begging you, help me get her back safely.'

Aidan could see that Clara's Aunt Esther had a tear in her eye, and he felt a lump in his own throat after Mrs Parkinson's plea.

She nodded to the class, then Mr Quigley shook hands with each of the Parkinsons. While the teacher was distracted Aidan turned and glanced around the classroom. Most of the pupils seemed to have been affected by what had been said, and even the Tobins looked a little chastened. But would anyone have any information? And if they had would they come forward? Aidan prayed that they would, but deep down he thought the chances weren't great, and he feared that his friend's life was still in danger.

Clara eavesdropped at the door of the barn. It was two days now since she had been kidnapped, and she had discovered that there was a living area attached to the wooden barn. It was in this adjoining room that her captors took turns in keeping guard. Clara had realised that by sitting right up at the door she could often hear their conversation.

Her mood had been fluctuating between fear and boredom. She wished she knew what progress was being made in the negotiation to free her, but all her captors would tell her was that they had offered the authorities her release in exchange for a reversal of the death sentence on Pat Brennan. Fighting inwardly to keep her fears at bay, Clara had told herself that it wasn't an outlandish demand – they weren't, after all, insisting that the condemned man be freed – and she hoped that the authorities would agree to the appeal and drop the death penalty.

When she wasn't grappling with her fears Clara's other big problem was boredom. Using a hair clip, she had tried to pick the lock on the wooden chest. Unlike in the adventure stories that she read, it wasn't easily done, and after failing to make any progress she had hidden the chest again under the hay. Meanwhile she had nothing to read, no instrument to play and the hours had passed slowly. To occupy herself, Clara had relived in her head different summer holidays with her family. She mentally travelled back in time, trying to recall each day of the holiday in sequence, and remembering the sights, sounds and smells of those happier times.

The highlights of each day, however, had been mealtimes. Her captors had fed her well, and aside from the food, she appreciated even the limited conversation with her masked guards as they delivered her meals. Clara had hoped she might overhear something that would give a clue as to who the men were, or where she was being detained, especially as they wouldn't have been expecting her to sit right at the door listening for any indiscretion. So far, however, they had let nothing slip.

Clara had been saving a piece of chocolate that had come on her lunch tray, and now she decided to treat herself. She was about to rise from where she was sitting at the barn door when her attention was suddenly caught by the sound of an approaching rider. There was the fast pounding of hooves, the sound growing louder before the horseman came to an abrupt stop. She heard an outside door opening, then the rider must have entered the adjoining room.

'Well?' her guard asked.

'Bad news,' said the new arrival breathlessly. 'They turned down the appeal. The hanging is going ahead!'

'Damn!' said the first man. 'Damn them anyway!'

'Yeah.'

'So what do we do now?'

'We have to show them that we're serious about the girl. It's our only hope.'

Clara bit her lip trying to dampen the terror she felt. But there was no getting away from it. This was really bad news – and her life was on the line.

Molly walked quickly out of the school yard, with Aidan following right behind her. As soon as they were away from the other pupils, she spoke urgently. 'We have to try again with your uncle.'

'I know. I was hoping that after what the Parkinsons said, someone might come forward.'

'So was I.'

'No one in the class seems to know anything, though,' said Aidan. 'Or if they do, they're afraid to speak.'

'We should go straight to the cottage now. And this time if your uncle's not there we wait until he comes home. No matter how long it takes.'

'He mightn't come home till later tonight.'

'Then we'll be waiting for him when he does.'

'I'm on to do this, but…what about our families, if we're gone missing till tonight?' said Aidan.

Mollie thought a moment. 'You've a bedroom to yourself, haven't you?'

'Yes.'

'OK, so we both quickly drop off our schoolbags. But you also write a note and leave it on your pillow saying where we're gone. Then get out fast before you're seen. If we're back from your uncle's cottage in plenty of time you can tear it up, if we're not, they'll eventually find the note and know where we've gone.'

'Will you write one too?' asked Aidan.

'No, my little sister might find it. We don't want anyone knowing where we've gone until we've done what we have to.'

'Fair enough.'

'Oh no,' said Molly, coming to a sudden halt. 'No!'

'What is it?' asked Aidan.

They had reached the main street of Ballydowd and Molly pointed to Larkins, a shop that sold newspapers as well as groceries and hardware. On the newspaper stand was a stop press headline. BRENNAN APPEAL REJECTED.

'That's bad for Clara,' said Aidan.

'Very bad.'

'You're right, we really need to tackle Uncle Sean.'

Molly nodded. 'Let's dump our bags then, and get out there.'

CHAPTER THIRTY-EIGHT

Garrett silently gave thanks, yet again, that Mam had come with him today. He knew he would never have been able to persuade the sacristan in Ballydowd to go to all of the trouble she had undertaken if he had arrived by himself. And he wouldn't have had the money or the self-assurance to order a taxi to take them from Ballydowd to Mullingar, as Mam had done without a second thought.

They were now in Mullingar library, going through microfiche records of old copies of *The Westmeath Examiner* newspaper. The word 'tragic' on the family headstone had set Mam's mind thinking, and now she and Garrett were seeking Ballydowd-related stories from 1881 that had the word 'tragic' in their title.

Garrett felt nervous, sensing that they might be on the brink of a breakthrough, yet knowing that if they found nothing there would be a big sense of anti-climax after all of this effort.

'Oh my God!' his mother suddenly exclaimed.

'What is it?' said Garrett, turning immediately to face her. Garrett was taken aback by the stunned expression on Mam's face. 'What is it, Mam?' he asked more gently.

His mother looked up from the article. 'Oh God, Garrett,' she said. 'Tragic is the word all right.'

'What have you found?'

'Read it for yourself,' she said. 'Read it for yourself...'

CHAPTER THIRTY-NINE

'Aidan,' said Uncle Sean in surprise, 'what brings you out here?'

Aidan took a breath, trying to get up his nerve. He had gone to the back door of the cottage, knocked briefly then stepped inside the scullery. His uncle had been writing at the kitchen table, but had risen quickly, covered the paperwork, and stepped forward.

Aidan hadn't entered the kitchen proper, but stood unmoving in the draughty scullery and looked Sean in the eye. 'I want you...I want you to release Clara Parkinson,' he said.

Aidan watched his uncle carefully and he could see the shock in his eyes. 'I know you're involved,' Aidan quickly continued, wanting to press his advantage while Sean was off balance, 'and I want you to let her go.'

'I'm not involved,' said Sean. 'But even if I was, what's Clara Parkinson to you?'

'She's my friend.'

'What?'

'I'm not going into how it all happened, that doesn't matter now. But Clara is my friend.'

'Since when did the Dalys make friends with the enemy?'

'Clara's not the enemy. She's a twelve-year-old girl who's done nothing wrong. Please, Uncle Sean, just do the right thing and let her go – and I'll never tell anyone what I know.'

'You know nothing, son!' said Sean aggressively. 'And if you ever say any of this outside these four walls, you'll be a sorry boy!'

Aidan tried not to flinch, and he concentrated hard on not letting his voice waver. 'That's not the way it's going to work, Uncle Sean,' he said. 'I *know* you're involved. I found the dynamite and the handcuffs you had hidden.'

'You snooping brat!' cried Sean, stepping forward angrily and swinging his hand back to strike out.

'Go on then!' Aidan cried. Despite his fear, he forced himself not to draw back. 'Hit out – that's your answer to everything!'

Sean pulled back from the blow, but still looked furious. Aidan's heart was pounding. He was relieved not to have been struck, but he tried not to show it and instead held his uncle's gaze.

'The handcuffs were for kidnapping Clara, weren't they? You took her hostage, why can't you be man enough to admit it?'

'OK we took her hostage! Because Pat Brennan's life is at stake. But you're more worried about some spoiled little brat!'

'I hope Pat Brennan isn't hanged. But that's nothing to do with Clara. You have to let her go.'

'Do I, now?'

'Yes.'

'Or what?'

'Or I'll go to the RIC.'

'The RIC have been all over me. They can't prove anything.'

'I'll tell them about the dynamite and the handcuffs.'

'I'll deny it. Your word against mine. You'd be making an informer of yourself – the lowest form of life. And to no avail.'

'Not to no avail. I'd be freeing a friend who's completely innocent.'

'No one is completely innocent. She benefits from other people's misery.'

'She's twelve years old!'

Sean shrugged. 'Like I say, there's no proof, and it would be your word against mine.'

'Not just my word. I've a witness.' Aidan turned around and called out. 'Molly!'

Turning back around, he could see the confusion in his uncle's face as Molly opened the back door and stepped in.

'I listened to every word at the door,' she said. 'And I'll testify that you admitted kidnapping Clara.'

'Molly is a friend of Clara's too,' explained Aidan. 'The game is up, Uncle Sean. Unless we do a deal.'

'A deal?'

'Yes. If you let Clara go, we'll say nothing.'

Aidan could see that his uncle's mind was racing, and he swallowed hard, hoping that Sean would agree.

'No,' said his uncle. 'I'd have no guarantee. I could free her, and then you could turn me in.'

'We wouldn't. We'll both swear on our mother's lives that we'll keep our word if you let Clara go.'

For a moment Sean said nothing and seemed to be lost in

thought, then he slowly turned back and looked Aidan in the eye. 'All right then,' he said reluctantly. 'Swear.'

'I swear on my mother's life,' said Aidan, 'that I won't inform on you if you let Clara go.'

'And I swear on my mother's life that I won't inform on you if you let Clara go,' said Molly.

'But we'd need to see Clara actually being released,' cautioned Aidan.

Sean seemed to think some more, then nodded. 'All right,' he answered, sounding angry but resigned. He crossed to the kitchen table and gathered up some papers which he folded and slipped into his jacket pocket, then he returned to Aidan and Molly.

'Come on then,' he said abruptly. 'It's an hour's journey; we need to go.'

Clara could hardly believe her ears. Much of the time there was only one person guarding her, which made it pointless to sit at the barn door eavesdropping. Now though, she had moved quickly to the door on hearing a horse and cart arriving in the farmyard. But the last people on earth whose voices she expected to hear were Aidan and Molly. *What was going on?*

The person they were talking to was the leader of her captors, and Clara heard him saying, 'She's in the barn.' Clara swallowed hard. It seemed almost inconceivable, yet the thought entered her mind. *Could Aidan and Molly somehow be in on her kidnapping?* Surely not, she reasoned, they had become such good friends. There must be some other explanation, she told herself, though she struggled to imagine what it might be.

Before she could think about it any further, she heard the sound of the door being unlocked and she stepped back, not wanting her captors to know that she listened in on their conversations. The door swung open, and Molly and Aidan entered the barn, followed by the leader of the kidnappers. Molly was surprised to see that he wasn't wearing his mask, but before she could think about what that meant, Aidan spoke.

'We're here to free you,' he said with a broad smile.

Clara was dumbfounded, but she saw Molly smiling also.

'It's true, you're being released,' she said.

'Oh my God!' said Clara, her eyes welling up with tears. She felt a huge wave of relief, and before she knew what she was doing she ran to Molly and threw her arms around her. She had no idea how her friends had found her, or why she was being let go. But she felt profoundly grateful, and guilty for having doubted them, however briefly.

Molly let her go, and Clara turned to Aidan and hugged him also. 'What happened?' she said, 'how did you...?'

'It's a long story,' said Aidan, 'but the main thing is it's over now.'

'Well...not exactly,' said the man.

'What do you mean?' said Aidan.

'Your little rescue mission ends here.'

'What are you saying?' demanded Molly.

'You wanted to see your friend, the prisoner. Well, now you have. And you can join her as prisoners yourselves till we get this execution halted.'

'We made a deal!' cried Aidan.

'And now the deal is off,' said the man.

Clara felt a stab of despair. To have had freedom within her grasp only to have it suddenly withdrawn was soul-destroying. She had no idea what Aidan and Molly had agreed to with this man for her release, but whatever it was he was clearly double-crossing them.

'You gave us your word!' said Aidan. 'You lied through your teeth!'

'And you were stupid enough to believe it.'

'You have no...you have no honour!' said Molly

The man rounded on her angrily. 'I can't afford honour! I'm trying to save a man's life!'

'How do you think you're ever going to get away with this?' said Aidan. 'Molly and I know who you are.' He turned to Clara. 'This is my uncle, believe it or not.'

Clara was shocked, but said nothing as Aidan turned back to his uncle. 'We know who you are, I know the fella outside is Mike Shanley from Mullingar. Unless you're planning to kill us all, how do you expect to get away with this?'

'Mike and I are making a fresh start, away from this godforsaken county. We're going to America, and we'll never be found there. But before we go, we'll strike one last blow. And by God, if we don't save Pat Brennan's life it won't be for want of trying!' The man turned away from Aidan and pointed threateningly at Clara. 'And you,' he said, 'you're going to write a letter pleading for your life, in return for Pat Brennan's.' He took sheets of paper and a pencil from his jacket pocket, placing them on top of the hay. 'I've written it down. You copy it out in your own hand, word for word.'

Clara was frightened, but she felt angry too and her temper flared. 'Write it yourself!'

The man drew nearer, reaching into his pocket and taking out a gun. He aimed it at Clara, then spoke in a voice that was even more chilling for being soft-spoken.

'No matter what happens, I won't kill my own nephew, traitor and all that he is. And I won't even kill the daughter of an RIC man. But you're a little parasite from a family of parasites. And if it costs your life to save my comrade, believe me, I won't think twice.' He indicated the paper and pencil. 'I'll give you ten minutes. If you want to live, write the letter – and hope it works.'

CHAPTER FORTY

'This is amazing,' said Garrett.

'I know,' answered Mam. 'But it's all there in black and white. We're descended from an RIC family.'

Garrett sat stunned in Mullingar library beside the microfiche machine that displayed back editions of *The Westmeath Examiner*. He could see a blue sky outside the window, and the room was warm from the March sunshine, but Garrett was oblivious to his surroundings.

'Why would Granny be so keen to cover that up?' he asked.

'Probably because when the Land War broke out, our ancestors found themselves on the wrong side. Even years later, after we got independence, no one wanted to draw attention to having served with the RIC.'

'But we're talking about stuff that happened in 1881 – before Granny was even born.'

Mam shrugged. 'She probably heard whispers about it all when she was a girl.'

'You reckon?'

'I'd say so. Though sometimes people dealt with tragedy by not talking openly about it.'

'We should talk to Granny when we go back,' said Garrett. 'Tell her we know it all now, and there's no need for keeping it to herself any longer.'

'Yes. Maybe even lay the ghosts to rest, by bringing her back to Ballydowd graveyard. We could all pay our respects together.'

'I'd like that,' said Garrett. 'Do you think Granny would be on for it?'

'I hope so,' said Ma. 'It would be nice to bring a peaceful end to a violent story.'

'Yes,' said Garrett quietly. 'Yes, it would.'

CHAPTER FORTY-ONE

'I have a plan,' said Molly. 'It's…it's a bit risky, but it could free us all.'

'What is it?' said Aidan.

Clara had been writing out the letter, but she put down the pencil and paper and looked up enquiringly.

'I've just come up with it, so it's not all worked out,' answered Molly. 'But I got an idea when I heard the other fella leaving.'

'Mike Shanley?'

'Yes. With your uncle here on his own, it gives us a chance.'

'To do what?' asked Clara.

'To escape. It's now or never. Once you give over the letter, everything's out of our hands.'

'So what's your plan?' asked Aidan.

'They gave Clara a candle and matches.' Molly pointed at the hay that was stacked high around the walls. 'We use the matches to set fire to the hay.'

Aidan looked incredulous. 'We set fire to a barn that we're locked into?'

'Yes,' said Molly. 'He'll never expect that. But your uncle isn't going to let us all burn to death. So he'll open the door.'

'And then what?' asked Clara.

'His attention will be on the fire,' answered Molly. 'And on you,

Clara, because you'll be screaming in terror. While he's distracted, we pounce from behind the door, and hit him on the head with the water bucket. We might have to hit him a few times to knock him out. Then we drag him to safety and we escape in the horse and cart.'

'That's...it's certainly daring...' said Clara.

Molly could see that both of her friends were taken aback by her suggestion, but she was encouraged by the fact that Clara wasn't rejecting it. Aidan looked more dubious, however.

'Supposing the fire gets out of hand?' he said.

'He's your flesh and blood, Aidan. He'll open the door before it gets to that.'

'And supposing we don't overpower him?'

'We have to.'

'He's big, and strong, and tough,' said Aidan.

'But we'll have the element of surprise,' countered Molly. 'I don't like violence, but Clara's life is at stake. So I'll smash him on the head with a metal bucket if that's what it takes.'

Molly could see that Aidan was weighing things up. 'It's...it's pretty risky,' he said.

'I know,' she answered. 'But even if we fail, things will be no worse than they are now. And the fire might draw attention, and get us released that way. Look, I know it's not perfect, but it could work.'

There was a pause, then Clara nodded. 'You're right,' she said, 'it's worth a try. Count me in.'

'Aidan?'

He hesitated another moment then seemed to reach a decision. 'All right. I'm in too.'

'Good,' said Molly. 'OK then, we need to work out who does what.'

Clara took deep breaths to try to dampen her fear. Mixed in with the fear was a surge of affection and admiration for Molly and Aidan. It was hard to believe that they had been friends for just a few months, yet here they were putting themselves at risk on her behalf. She found it hard not to feel guilty, but she told herself that if the situation were reversed, she would do the same for them. She turned to them now, trying hard to keep her voice sounding calm.

'There's something…there's something I want to say.'

'Yes?' said Aidan.

'I…I really appreciate all you've done to try to save me. You're… you're just the best friends anyone could ever have…' Clara found her voice cracking with emotion, and her eyes welled up with tears. 'Sorry, I didn't mean to…I just…thank you *so much*.'

Aidan reached out and squeezed her arm. 'One for all and all for one, Clara,' he said, managing a quick smile despite the circumstance.

Clara tried for a smile in return, then Molly approached and hugged her tightly.

'You're a great friend too,' said Molly softly, 'and we'll all get out of this together.'

'We will,' said Clara, feeling her resolve stiffening.

Molly released her, and Clara turned to her friends. 'All right then, are we ready?'

'Yes,' said Aidan.

'Yes,' said Molly.

Clara crossed to the door and listened to make sure that Aidan's uncle was in the other room.

'He's there,' she said softly as she re-crossed the barn, lifted the box of matches and took one out. She bit her lip, willing herself to action. Then she struck the match, watched it burst into flame and set alight the nearest pile of hay.

Aidan gripped the pitchfork tightly and tried to stop the trembling in his limbs. He was shocked at how rapidly the fire was spreading through the hay, but even more frightening was the idea of assaulting his uncle. Fighting and aggression had never come naturally to Aidan, but he knew he couldn't let his friends down and that now he had to be brave.

It had been agreed that they would let the fire take a reasonable hold before Clara started screaming, and that Molly and Aidan would be the ones to take Sean by surprise with a two-pronged assault. As the bigger and stronger of the two Aidan had volunteered to strike the first blow when Sean entered. He would use the heavy wooden handle of the pitchfork, after which Molly would follow up, using the metal bucket as a weapon. Aidan tried to convince himself that the presence in the barn of a potential weapon like the pitchfork meant that his uncle had never considered that he might face resistance. But would surprise alone be enough to tilt the scales in their favour?

Aidan's thoughts were interrupted when the flames began to leap toward the ceiling and Molly called out in a low urgent voice. 'Start screaming, Clara! Start screaming!'

'Help!' roared Clara. 'A fire has started! Help us! Please, help us!'

The flames crackled and began to roar and Aidan hoped that he hadn't misjudged how quickly the barn might burn.

'Help!' screamed Clara. 'Fire! Help us! The barn's on fire!'

The fire was swiftly spreading through the dry hay, and Clara screamed with even more urgency as the harsh smell of smoke grew stronger. Aidan swallowed hard, praying that they hadn't made a fatal miscalculation. Molly had started shouting for help also, then after several more seconds – that seemed like an age – Aidan heard the door being unlocked from the other side.

He felt his pulses pounding, and his knees were trembling, but he gripped the pitchfork firmly, knowing that how he behaved in the next couple of moments could have life and death consequences. The door swung open and Sean stepped into the barn. The hay was blazing now, and he paused briefly, obviously shocked by the sight.

Aidan knew that this was his moment. But Sean was violent, and possibly armed, and it could all go horribly wrong. Aidan hesitated. Then he saw Clara's frightened face and he overcame his fear and leaped forward. The barn door had partially shielded Aidan, and Sean didn't see the attack coming. Just as his uncle was starting to move forward, Aidan drove the wooden handle of the pitchfork into his stomach with all his might. Sean doubled up, his face contorted with shock and pain. Aidan saw that the blow to his solar plexus had winded him. But it hadn't brought him to his knees. Gripping his stomach, Sean started to straighten up. Molly suddenly sprang forward, swinging the metal bucket with all her strength. In spite of everything Aidan grimaced when the bucket made contact with his uncle's head. Sean staggered and fell to his knees, and Molly swung again and landed another heavy blow. This time Sean collapsed to the ground.

'Go, Clara! Get the cart!' cried Aidan. Clara ran out the door, and Aidan dropped to his knees and quickly patted his uncle's pockets in case he had the gun on him.

'Traitor!' muttered Sean groggily.

Aidan ignored the accusation. 'He hasn't the gun on him!'

'It's probably in the kitchen!' said Molly. 'Let's go!'

Sean was sprawled on the floor, badly dazed from the blows to the head, but the three friends had agreed that it would be important to try to find Sean's weapon during their escape bid – for all they knew they might encounter some of the other men returning.

'OK,' said Aidan, rising from his hunkers

'The chest,' cried Sean feebly, 'the chest!'

Aidan ignored him and ran with Molly out of the blazing barn
and into the kitchen of the adjoining cottage. He had hoped that
the weapon might be on the table or some other obvious place,
but there was no sign of it.

'Where the hell did he put it?' said Aidan.

'Who knows? But I can hear Clara bringing around the cart.
Should we just go?'

'All right, give me another few seconds while we're waiting on
her.'

'OK,' said Molly. 'I thought your uncle would crawl out of the
barn. I'll nip in and drag him out while you look for the gun.'

'Fine!' said Aidan

Molly ran back toward the barn, and Aidan heard Sean's voice
calling out above the sound of the flames. 'The chest! The dynamite chest!' Aidan swung around to see Molly disappearing into
the barn. Then there was an ear-splitting explosion. Aidan saw a
dazzling flash of light, and an instant later everything went silent
and dark.

CHAPTER FORTY-TWO

Weak January sunshine cast a pallid light through the bare branches of the trees as Clara and her mother walked through the hospital grounds. They made their way slowly towards the entrance, both of them wearing black hats, gloves, coats and long dresses, as was customary during a period of mourning. It was three days now since the explosion at the barn, and for Clara the time had been a nightmarish blur of police questioning, funerals and overwhelming sadness.

They entered the main door, and Clara's nostrils were hit by the hospital smell of antiseptic mixed with stuffy air.

'I think this time I should go with you, Clara,' said her mother.

'No, Mama, please. I have to do this alone.'

'But—'

'Please, Mama. I couldn't talk properly to Aidan yesterday. He kept drifting off because of the medicine he's on. I need...I need to talk to him by myself. You can thank him for saving me when he's stronger. But today can I see him alone?'

Her mother nodded slowly. 'All right, dear. I'll wait for you here.'

'Thank you, Mama.'

Clara watched her mother taking a seat in the lobby, then she headed off down the corridor. Her family had been through a maelstrom of emotions in the previous few days, with her parents hugely relieved that Clara had escaped uninjured, but shocked that she had carried out a secret friendship behind their backs. They had been horrified to hear that the ringleader of the kidnappers was Aidan's uncle, but Aunt Esther had countered that by pointing out that Aidan had heroically risked his life to save Clara.

Clara herself had been numbed with shock and she still felt in a daze, frequently reliving in her head the events of the last few days. She had been thrilled when Aidan and Molly had arrived to free her, and disgusted by the betrayal of Aidan's uncle that had made prisoners of her friends. She had been hugely moved by their loyalty, and by their bravery in fighting to release her. Mostly though, she was heartbroken by the loss of Molly. Her death, in the explosion that also took the life of Aidan's uncle Sean, had turned Clara's life upside down. She had been overwhelmed by grief, and anger, and guilt that Molly had died because of her. The rational part of her brain knew that it wasn't her fault that she had been kidnapped, and that Molly had been killed by illegally-held dynamite that was hidden in the chest in the barn. But it had still been hard to shake off a feeling of responsibility for her friend, and Clara had sobbed uncontrollably at Molly's funeral and slept badly for the last new nights.

She paused now outside the door to Aidan's room, gathering herself. Most of the patients in the hospital were housed in wards, but there was a corridor of private rooms, and Papa had insisted on having Aidan privately treated at his expense, as a gesture of thanks for rescuing his daughter.

Clara knocked softly, then entered. To her relief, Aidan was sitting up in bed and looking more, alert than the previous day.

'Clara,' he said.

'Aidan,' she answered in greeting, placing a bunch of black grapes that she had brought on the bedside locker and sitting in the chair beside his bed. 'How are you today?'

'Not too bad.' He gave a weak grin. 'I think I was dozing off a fair bit when you were here before. Sorry.'

'That's fine.' Although his head was bandaged and his left arm was in a splint, Clara was relieved that Aidan seemed far stronger today. 'You're looking much better,' she said.

'I feel much better. Well…I feel…I feel *terrible* when I think about Molly…'

'Me too.' said Clara, her voice breaking. 'Me too, Aidan.' She reached out and squeezed his uninjured arm, trying hard to hold back her tears. He nodded, and they both sat unmoving for a moment, then Clara turned to face him, dabbing her eyes dry with a handkerchief. 'There's something I wanted to say,' she began tentatively.

'Yes?'

'I wanted to say it yesterday, but you were drifting in and out.'

'So… what is it?'

'I just wanted to say thank you from the bottom of my heart. I think you were incredibly brave. First you came looking for me, and then you took on a man twice your size. I'll never forget that,

Aidan. Never.'

Clara could see that her friend was moved, and he hesitated as though trying to find the right words.

'Thanks, Clara, that…that means a lot. But…but I feel I should apologise.'

'Apologise? For what?'

'For my uncle. I suppose I should say "God rest him", now he's dead, but I can't. None of this would have happened if it wasn't for him.'

'You're not responsible for your uncle.'

'I know. But he was part of my family, and…and he was a fanatic.' Aidan looked at her, then spoke plaintively. 'Why do fanatics always think they're right, and that that excuses anything?'

'I suppose…I suppose they feel the end justifies the means,' said Clara.

'But it doesn't, does it? It destroyed Molly's family, and caused huge worry to yours. And in the end it might have killed you.'

'But he didn't kill me, because you and Molly saved me. So please, don't ever apologise again. You and Molly were the best friends anyone could ask for, and I owe you my life.'

Aidan didn't respond, but Clara sensed that he had taken in what she said. 'I've never had friends like that before,' she said. 'And I've you to thank for it. I'll never forget the last few months, they've been brilliant. And if I live to be a hundred, I won't forget Molly. I'll cherish her memory till the day I die.'

'So will I,' said Aidan.

'Let's...let's make it a pact,' suggested Clara. 'On the day she died – on the 17th January every year – no matter what else is going on in our lives, we'll think about her. Maybe say a little prayer.'

Aidan nodded. 'Knowing Molly, she wouldn't want it to be too sad, though. So let's remember the good times we had too, and how much fun she was.'

'Yes, that sounds...that sounds about right,' said Clara.

'OK, then, that's what we'll do every year.'

'OK.'

Aidan looked at her, and held out his uninjured arm. Clara rose from the chair and reached out to her friend. She moved carefully, aware of his injuries, and they hugged tenderly, without the need to say another word.

CHAPTER FORTY-THREE

The warm, spring air was sweet with the scent of flowers, and the only sound was the soft singing of the birds as Garrett stood with his family in Ballydowd graveyard. How peaceful it all seemed today, he thought, yet this had been the scene of heartbreak and drama for his ancestors in 1881.

Now Garrett had returned to Ballydowd with Mam, Dad, and Granny, and despite the family tragedy that had unfolded one hundred and fifty years previously, there was a pleasing sense of closure about returning today to pay their respects.

He stood before the headstone that detailed the tragic death of his great-great-grand-aunt, Molly O'Hara, whose little sister Helen had gone on to marry Granny's grandfather, Thomas Donnelly. It felt like they had come full circle as a family, and Garrett was glad that Granny had been relieved of the burden of keeping things secret.

He understood how covering up an RIC past and not wanting to dwell on a tragedy made sense to past generations of his family. But it had felt like a healthier approach when Granny had admitted the truth while shedding a few tears, and had then agreed to accompany them here today. She had led them in a short prayer for her grand-aunt Molly, and now she lifted the wreath of red roses that they had brought with them to lay on the grave.

To Garrett's surprise she turned to him and looked him in the eye.

'Thank you,' she said softly.

'For...for what, Granny?'

'For persevering, and eventually bringing us all to here.' She held out the wreath. 'Let's lay it together.'

Garrett hadn't expected the gesture and he felt a slight lump in his throat. 'I'd be honoured,' he said. Taking one side of the wreath, he stepped forward with his grandmother and laid it on the grave.

'Rest in peace, Molly,' said Granny softly, 'rest in peace.'

'Amen,' said Garrett. Then he linked arms with his grand-mother, re-joined his parents, and slowly walked away through the quiet of the sunlit graveyard.

EPILOGUE

Clara's parents continued to live on the Parkinson Estate, but her Aunt Esther married and moved to Canada when her new husband was offered a posting there. Clara went to boarding school, then studied music in London. She never became an orchestra performer, but on returning to Ireland she married and settled happily in Dublin, where for many years she ran a highly-regarded music school. She didn't live again on the Parkinson Estate, much of which was sold in time to local farmers, and in the 1940s the house and the rest of the estate passed out of the ownership of the Parkinson family. Today the house and remaining grounds operate as a hotel and spa.

Despite the tragic loss of Molly, Sergeant O'Hara remained in the Royal Irish Constabulary until he reached pension age. By then his younger daughter Helen had met a local cooper, Thomas Donnelly, whom she would eventually marry in Ballydowd before moving to Dublin when Thomas got a job in the Guinness brewery. Molly's mother never fully got over the death of her daughter, but she carried on working as a seamstress, and in time found consolation and happiness in her role as grandmother to Helen's children.

Iggy Tobin emigrated to Chicago where he worked for the rest of his life as a labourer in the stock yards. His twin brother Peadar was killed on the railway line near Ballydowd when he drunkenly tried to cross the line and was struck by a goods train.

The Daly family eventually came to own the land on which they farmed, thanks to a government loan scheme. Aidan, however, stayed true to his dream, leaving rural life behind to work in the clothing industry. He became an expert in textiles and tailoring and eventually became the head buyer in an upmarket department store in Manchester. He married and had a family in England. But every year on 17 January he met up with Clara in Dublin. They had lunch together, after which they went through the entries and picked the winning candidate for the Molly O'Hara Memorial Scholarship that Clara awarded annually for free tuition in her music school. Then they said a short prayer for Molly, before raising their glasses in a toast – to a friend they would never forget.

HISTORICAL NOTE

The Bessborough Commission reported back to the government in Westminster in January 1881, recommending major land reforms, and later that month, Charles Stewart Parnell, the leader of the Irish Party, was released from prison. In April Prime Minister Gladstone introduced the Land Law Act, which gave basic rights to tenant farmers. Land courts were set up that would fix fair rents for a period of fifteen years, giving farm families security for the first time. The campaigns of the Land League and Irish Party were regarded as having delivered a major victory, the first in a longer political battle that would lead eventually to many tenant farmers getting to own the land that they worked.

Captain Boycott never returned to Lough Mask estate in County Mayo, but his name entered the English language, and the verb 'boycott', meaning to refuse to have any dealings with someone or something, had by 1888 been listed as a word in *A New English Dictionary on Historic Principals* – later known as the *Oxford English Dictionary*.

The Royal Irish Constabulary was disbanded in 1922 with the founding of the Irish Free State, and a new police force, the Civic Guard, renamed the following year as An Garda Síochána, replaced the RIC.

Winds of Change is a work of fiction, and the families of Clara, Aidan, Molly, and Garrett are figments of my imagination. Mullingar is a large town in County Westmeath, still served today by both the rail line and the Royal Canal, Ashtown is a suburb of Dublin, and *The Westmeath Examiner* is an actual newspaper, but Ballydowd and the Parkinson Estate are fictitious locations.

Broadstone Railway Station, where Clara arrived with her mother and aunt, is a real location in Dublin. It closed to passenger traffic in 1937, and today its track bed is used by the Luas tram system.

Brian Gallagher,
Dublin 2020

READ MORE GREAT BOOKS

by Brian Gallagher

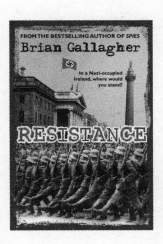

In Nazi-occupied Ireland, Roisin Tierney hides her Jewish heritage. But when the chance arises to resist the Nazis, Roisin and her friends face hard choices - that could cost their lives.

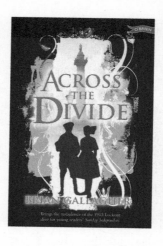

When Liam and Nora meet at a Feis Ceol, an unlikely bond is formed - a bond that leads to a friendship spanning the deeply divided city that was Dublin in 1913.

Friends Emer and Jack are on opposite sides in a life and death struggle, when Dublin city is torn apart in the 1916 Easter Rising. With their young lives in turmoil, what will come first – friendship, family or loyalty to a cause?

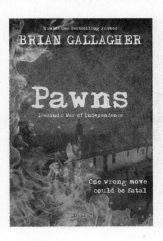

During the War of Independence, friends Johnny, Stella and Alice grapple with conflicting loyalties – then matters come dramatically to a head on the night the Black and Tans set Balbriggan ablaze during a murderous night of vengeance.

As the War of Independence grows more lethal, the three friends must decide where their loyalties lie. Then a secret from Johnny's past changes everything…

Dublin, 1922. Annie Reilly's friend Peter sides with the rebels in the Civil War. When Annie's life is threatened, he has to decide where his loyalties lie.

1941. Grace and Barry begin to suspect their teacher Mr Pawlek of spying for the Nazis. But what starts as an exciting adventure puts their lives in danger.